Rollins of Riverview 3

~*~*~*~*~*~*~*~*~*~

Unconditional Suitor

~*~*~*~*~*~*~*~*~*~

A Novella

By Daphanie Ann Austin

Daphanie Ann Austin

Rollins of Riverview, Unconditional Suitor

Books by Daphanie Ann Austin

Rollins of Riverview

Angel Ranger

The Half-Breeds Bride

Unconditional Suitor

Daphanie Austin is a full time house wife to her husband Jerry, and a devoted mother to their three precious children Aaron, Wyatt and Hannah. She is a budding author with a fierce devotion to God, her family and her Yorkie, Lexi. She enjoys sewing, web design, photography, reading and of course writing. Daphanie loves history and has a vivid, passionate imagination that she loves to put on paper. Her books aren't typical of Christian romance books. She loves clean, passionate romance and her books reflect her passion. She believes Christians are human and as such we are passionate creatures too. We just choose to show restraint in ours. She and her family make their temporary, earthly home in America's heartland.

This third book is dedicated to three special ladies who fueled
my love of reading and inspired me to write.

First is my wonderful Grandma, Jaunita. Thank you Grandma for your love and support. It is such a joy to share books back and forth with you.
The second is Mrs. Kristi. For all your crazy, wonderful ways and for being the first person to introduce me to Christian romance novels.
Last, but not least is Ms. Chris. You're not only a kindred spirit in reading, but thank you for being so generous with your precious books!

Prologue

September 1874

Eight year old, Trevor Lee Rollins trudged begrudgingly to his school desk. The only highlight of the first day being back was that now it was in the second row of desks instead of the first. That row was reserved for the beginners and he was proud to be in his second year.

After plunking himself unceremoniously into his desk chair he turned around in search of his brother and sister.

Katie was easy to spot since she was only two years behind him in school and therefore only two rows behind him in class. She gave him a little wave and a reassuring smile.

He was closer to Katie than he was to his brother. She was closer to his age and they played together a lot. Though he would never admit that little bit of information to his chums. A man had a certain image to keep up after all.

Luke on the other hand was in his last year and was sitting in the last row. When Trevor finally did spot him he was too busy chatting with his friends and flirting with the girls to pay him any mind.

'Girls!' Trevor almost snorted out loud at the spectacle his brother was making of himself. Trevor didn't see what all the fuss was about. As far as he was concerned they all giggled too much, and smelled funny.

'Why, they can't even fish or hunt!' Trevor thought shaking his head in disgust. What his brother saw in the frilly creatures was beyond his imagining.

As far as he was concerned his mother and sister seemed to be the only females with any sense at all.

The room grew silent as the school teacher, Mr. McGreggor, made his way to the front of the school room. Trevor liked his teacher. Mr. McGreggor didn't put up with any foolishness, but he loved his students and had the patience of Job.

"Good morning class!"

"Good morning Mr. McGreggor," the students' voices greeted in unison.

"I'm so glad to see so many familiar faces back in my classroom," the teacher informed them cheerfully, then turned his attention to the first row of nervous students. Trevor was glad to note that no one had taken the seat directly in front of him.

"I'm also glad to see new faces this morning," Mr. McGreggor continued. "I think the first thing we are going to do this morning is to get acquainted with one another. We'll start with the first row and work our way to the back of the room. Would you please stand up and introduce yourself?" he asked gesturing to a carrot topped, freckle faced little boy in the front row.

Trevor had to fight to keep from wrinkling his nose. He hated red hair and freckles!

It seemed like the introductions took forever and Trevor was relieved when the last boy in the last row finally sat down. He was ready to get this day over with. His dad had promised to take him fishing when he got home today and he had to fight not to fidget with anticipation.

"Thank you Billy," Mr. McGreggor said as the last student sat down. "Now that we are all acquainted…"

The sound of the school door opening sent heads turning in all directions and Trevor watched as a slim, redheaded woman poked her head into the room.

Trevor looked accusingly at the redheaded boy in the first row. What on earth could the woman want with her son so badly that it couldn't wait till after class!

"Excuse me," the woman said as she stepped fully into the room and blushed. "I'm sorry to interrupt."

"It's no problem," Mr. McGreggor rushed to assure her as he made his way toward the back of the room. "How can I help you?"

"Well, we're new to the area and I just found out at the mercantile that your class was starting today," the woman explained softly. "My daughter Jenny really needs to be in school. Is it too late to let her start today? I can bring her back tomorrow."

"No, no, there's no need to wait. She is more than welcome to start today," Mr. McGreggor assured her.

Trevor glared at the redheaded boy in the front row. How could a kid that ugly have the nerve to have a sister?!

"Oh! Thank you Mr…"

"McGreggor," the teacher filled in while smiling warmly at the woman, "I'm Mr. McGreggor."

"Thank you Mr. McGreggor. I'll just go get Jenny out of the wagon," the woman said and disappeared back out of the school door.

Trevor let out an impatient sigh as his teacher's feet seemed to be glued to the floor and his eyes glued to the door. This was going to be a long day.

Mr. McGreggor finally tore his gaze from the entrance and made his way back to the front of the class.

Trevor heard the door to the school open again and turned with everyone else to watch as the woman entered the room and turned back toward the door.

"Come along Jenny," she said firmly.

What happened next would be forever burned into Trevor's memory.

"Come on Honey," the woman coaxed while reaching out and grabbing a tiny hand.

Trevor watched transfixed as she pulled a redheaded, freckle faced girl through the doorway and fully inside the classroom, but this wasn't just any kind of red hair. No, this was the color of a new copper penny and as her mother led her to the front of the classroom the morning's rays streaming through the windows seemed to fight for the right to shine on the tightly coiled ringlets.

"Class, this is Jenny and she will begin her first year with us today," Mr. McGreggor said turning the girl to face the class.

Trevor was mesmerized. She had a smooth creamy complexion with just a light dusting of freckles across the bridge of her adorable upturned nose, but it was her eyes that were the real showpiece. Trevor's mother had a ring with a stone that color that his father had given her. When he'd asked his mother about it she'd told him it was topaz since she was born in November. Trevor had always loved that ring. The yellow, orange color of the stone reminded him of fall and fall was his favorite time of year.

Suddenly red hair and freckles didn't seem so bad. In fact he found that he suddenly loved red hair and freckles!

'Why, I might even befriend that ugly little kid in the front row,' he benevolently thought to himself.

"Have a good time Sweetie. I'll be back for you as soon as class is out," the girl's mother said giving her a quick hug and making a beeline for the door.

Trevor watched in horror as those big, beautiful topaz eyes filled with tears.

"There, there now," Mr. McGreggor soothed patting her awkwardly on the back. "Why don't you take a seat over here?" the teacher said leading her to the seat in front of Trevor.

He couldn't believe his good luck. When she sat down the smell of lilac surrounded him and he breathed deeply.

'Why can't all girls smell like that?' he thought to himself.

~*~*~*~

Jenny was terrified. She had never been away from her mother while she was awake before. She felt like everyone was looking at her, and she didn't like it so she tried to sink down as low as possible in her desk chair.

"Now, I am going to spend some time with the first row of students while the rest of you read the first lesson in your readers," Mr. McGreggor informed them all, and then addressed the first year students, "Now, if you will all follow me over to the corner table we'll begin learning the letter "A" today."

Jenny was loath to leave the safety of her desk, but she reluctantly eased out of her chair to obey her teacher. She had almost made it to the table he had indicated when Mr. McGreggor asked that they bring their slates, so she turned back for the piece of black slate and chalk her mother had purchased for her at the mercantile just minutes before she had brought her to school. As she bent down to pick up the needed items she felt a pair of eyes on her and glanced up to find a boy sitting directly behind her chair staring at her. An odd, unnamable sensation started at her toes and ended at the top of her head making her scalp tingle and her cheeks grow hot.

He was a handsome boy with short, dark blond hair and doe brown eyes. She absently noticed that he was the biggest boy in the second row and realized that he was only one year ahead of her in school.

Jenny didn't know how long she'd stood there staring at him, but she was absolutely mortified when the teacher had to clear his throat to get her attention. She chanced a quick glance at the boy once more and blushed to the roots of her hair when he gave her a wink. She spun around and quickly made her way to the corner table, but it was hard to concentrate with her mind still on the boy across the room. She was relieved when Mr. McGreggor finally announced that it was recess, but as soon as she realized she was going to have to interact with her fellow classmates the relief turned to terror.

She had never been around any children her age, or any age, before and she was nervous. It seemed like everything was changing so fast. She was glad her mom didn't have to work at that bad place anymore. Her mom promised her that life was going to be better for them from here on out, but Jenny had her doubts. After all it wasn't the first time her mom had tried to find a better job, but there just weren't many jobs for a single woman with a child.

Still Jenny had to admit that it was nice to know her mother was there while she slept now, and even nicer to be able to play during the day without the worry of waking her mother. Though her mother had never scolded Jenny when she had wakened her it bothered the little girl. She knew her mother needed rest too.

"Aren't you going to go play?" Mr. McGreggor's kind voice broke into her musings.

"I...I don't know," Jenny whispered softly.

"I tell you what," her teacher began while squatting down to her level, "I get awfully lonely out there without anyone to talk to. Would you just come out and visit with me?"

Jenny looked up into the teacher's kind hazel eyes in wonder. "You get lonely too?"

"I sure do," he replied, "so I find it best to have a friend to visit with. Will you come and visit with me?"

"Yes sir," Jenny beamed at her first friend in school.

"Wonderful! Thank you very much Jenny," her teacher exclaimed as he reached out and took her tiny hand in his.

Jenny allowed him to lead her toward the entrance and out into the school yard where her fellow classmates were already playing. Mr. McGreggor led her under a huge pecan tree and sat down in the grass to watch his students play. Jenny plopped down beside him and smiled.

"I am glad you and your parents moved here," Mr. McGreggor smiled back.

"It's just me and my mom," Jenny admitted.

"Really?" Mr. McGreggor asked, "Where is your dad?"

"I don't know," Jenny shrugged her small, slender shoulders, "I've never met him."

"He left your mom?" her teacher asked incredulously.

"No, he refused to marry her, so it's just the two of us," she informed him missing the look of horror that crossed his features. "Who is that?" Jenny asked pointing to the boy she'd seen earlier.

"That's Trevor Rollins," her teacher answered after coming out of his shock. "Listen Jenny," her teacher said taking her hand to gain her attention, "it's probably best if you don't mention the part about your dad to anyone else. Okay?"

"Why?" Jenny asked clearly confused.

"Well…" he thought for a moment, "I just think that's personal and is something your mom should tell if she wants to."

"Oh, okay Mr. McGreggor. I won't tell anyone else," she promised.

"Good girl," her teacher replied.

"Hello," they both heard a boys voice interrupt and Jenny looked up to find the boy Mr. McGreggor had identified as Trevor Rollins standing in front of them.

"Hello Trevor," Mr. McGreggor said smiling at him.

"I was wondering…well, I was hoping that maybe," Trevor ducked his head bashfully, "if Jenny would like to play with me?"

"Well, Trevor, that's up to Jenny," Mr. McGreggor said and looked at Jenny expectantly.

"Oh, I don't know," Jenny blushed and looked up at Trevor, "I promised Mr. McGreggor that I would keep him company."

"And so you have Jenny," the teacher informed her and gave her hand a reassuring squeeze, "but now I have some things inside that need my attention. Why don't you go play with Trevor for a while?"

Jenny hesitated only a moment more before smiling shyly up at the boy in front of her.

"Okay."

~*~*~*~

September 1879

~ 14 ~

Trevor scarfed down his breakfast and flew up the stairs to finish readying for school. He hadn't seen Jenny all summer and he was anxious to get to his first day of class.

He had been working and saving all summer and he was excited to show Jenny the beautiful topaz ring he'd bought for her. His brother had teased him unmercifully, but Trevor didn't care. Jenny was worth it.

They had been virtually inseparable since that first day of school five years ago. Jenny had been his best friend and last year he'd finally worked up the nerve to ask her to be his girl. Their chums teased them about it at first, but neither cared. They were in love.

The short wagon ride to town seemed to take forever to a love sick school boy, and he baled out of the vehicle before it was able to come to a complete stop.

"Trevor," his mother's voice stopped him dead in his tracks just as he was about to make a mad dash for the school house. "You forgot your lunch Sweetheart."

"Oh!" Trevor rushed back to the wagon and accepted his lunch from his mother's outstretched hand. He was just about to dash off again when he abruptly turned, climbed into the front seat and gave his mother a peck on the cheek. "Thanks Momma. I love you."

"I love you too dear," his mother, Ruby, beamed at him. "Have a good day."

"It will be a wonderful day as long as Jenny's here," Trevor assured her as he leapt from the wagon and made a beeline for the door of the school house. Just as he was about to reach the entrance he heard a wagon and glanced toward the coming sound. The bright sunshine gleamed on the glorious copper curls of a girl sitting in the front seat of a wagon. A huge smile split Trevor's face.

"Jenny!" he called out as he bounded back down the school's steps.

"Trevor!" Jenny cried and stood up before the wagon had come to a complete stop.

"Jenny!" Mr. McGreggor's voice sounded beside her. "You need to wait till the wagon stops completely."

"Sorry Dad," Jenny repented, but grinned sheepishly.

Mr. McGreggor laughed at her and smiled at Trevor. "Hello Trevor. I think she is ready for school today," he sent the lad a wink, "I think she must really like her new teacher."

"No one can be as good as you were Daddy," she informed him as she bent down to peck his cheek just before reaching for Trevor.

"She's right Mr. McGreggor," Trevor agreed as he swung Jenny around and placed her on the ground.

"You two are just bias," Mr. McGreggor argued, "but I'm glad you think so. Now have a good day you two. Either me or your Momma will be waiting for you when class lets out Princess."

"I could walk her home Mr. McGreggor," Trevor volunteered.

"I don't know Trevor," Mr. McGreggor furrowed his eyebrows. "I'd have to talk to the Mrs. first. How about I talk to her and if she says yes you can walk her home tomorrow?"

"Okay Mr. McGreggor," Trevor beamed up at him, "Thank you!"

Mr. McGreggor watched as his step daughter placed her dainty hand in the crook of Trevor's arm and was escorted to class. He smiled and shook his head as he chucked to the horses and set off for home and his beautiful wife.

~*~*~*~

April 1880

Trevor and Jenny walked hand in hand toward the McGreggor farm. Jenny was glad the weather had finally warmed back up so Trevor could start walking her home again. She had worn his favorite dress for the occasion; a spring green calico dress with yellow accents. At only fourteen her mom said she was still too young to wear her hair up, so she tied the unruly curls back with a matching green ribbon.

All around them spring was popping up. Unfortunately the warmer weather also meant summer was right around the corner and Jenny wasn't looking forward to be separated from Trevor again.

"Jenny?" Trevor broke the companionable silence and pulled them both to a stop along the clay road. He waited until she looked up at him before continuing. "Will you marry me?"

"Right now?" Jenny asked in surprise, sure that her parents would never approve.

"No, not right now, but...well... I mean...will you promise to marry me one day?" Trevor asked as he tucked a stray strand of hair behind her ear. "I love you Jenny Lynn McGreggor."

"Oh Trevor! I love you too!" Jenny exclaimed as she reached out and placed one hand on his smooth cheek. "Of course I'll marry you."

"Do you promise?" Trevor asked as he placed a gentle kiss in her palm.

Jenny couldn't seem to draw a full breath. He had never kissed her before and the feel of his lips on her palm sent her pulse to racing.

Trevor looked into her eyes and took a small step towards her. Jenny's own feet followed suit of their own accord and she found her self mere inches from him. She refused to look up though and Trevor had to use the crook of his finger under her chin to bring her gaze to his.

"Do you promise Jenny?" he asked again and Jenny could feel his warm breath on her lips.

"I promise," she whispered just before Trevor's lips claimed hers.

~*~*~*~

May 1880

Trevor was sad that there were only two weeks left in his last year of school, but he had asked Jenny's dad if he could court her and he was thrilled when Mr. McGreggor agreed. At least now he could at least make house calls to see her. At first his dad hadn't taken him seriously when he'd asked to borrow the buggy to court Jenny, but his mother had convinced him that Trevor was indeed serious.

He would miss seeing her every day, but seeing her once a week was better than not seeing her at all.

He paced anxiously in front of the schoolhouse, listening for the sound of an approaching wagon, but every time he heard one it wasn't her. By the time school was ready to begin he was getting worried. Jenny had never been late before. Mr. McGreggor was a stickler for punctuality.

When the school bell rang out he had little choice, but to find his seat.

All day long the empty desk in front of his taunted him, and by the end of the day he had worked himself into a fine state.

As soon as the teacher dismissed them he made a beeline for his horse and tore off toward the McGreggor farm. He knew something wasn't right the moment he rode into the yard. The McGreggor milk cow, Maggie, bald pitifully as he walked by and Trevor noticed that her utters were painfully swollen from lack of milking. The chickens weren't in the yard either.

Trevor's pulse pounded in his ears as his fist pounded on the door.

A short, plump woman with frizzy, orange hair and a bird beak nose opened the door and sniffed disdainfully at him like he was some sort of rodent. "What do you want?"

"Um...well...I..." Trevor stuttered.

"Well, spit it out boy or go away!" the crotchety woman spat.

"I'm looking for Jenny," Trevor finally got out.

"She can't have no visitors right now," and with that she shut the door in his face.

Not to be detoured, Trevor started pounding on the door again. The door swung open and the woman glared at him.

"I done told you she can't have no visitors right now," she snarled. "She's in mourning."

"Can I talk to one of her parents then?" Surely the hateful woman couldn't deny him access to them.

"That's who she's in mourning for you daft, twit," she screeched and slammed the door once more.

Trevor stood there in a stunned stupor for a good long while before he walked with determined strides to where he knew Jenny's window was.

"Jenny!" he bellowed until he saw her figure appear in the window, but he only caught a fleeting glance before someone jerked her back. He was just about to start yelling for her again when he heard the sound of a gun being caulked. Trevor whirled toward the sound and came face to face with a round, bald man in his mid fifties. Trevor had a good six inches on the man, and he was broader and thicker than the man too, but the rifle the other man had leveled on him was a good equalizer, so Trevor raised his hands in surrender.

"I don't want any trouble," Trevor tried to reason with the man, "I just want to make sure Jenny is alright."

"I suggest you get on your horse and ride on out a' here," the man ground out.

Trevor had no choice, but to ride away. He sent one more glance toward the McGreggor farm as he turned onto the rode and saw Jenny standing at her parent's window. His heart broke as he saw her wiping tears away.

He had no way of knowing that, that would be the last time he would see her.

Chapter 1

April 1886

Trevor sat up in bed and blinked sleepily at the predawn light creeping in through his bedroom window, but he didn't see the sleepy little town slowly coming to life. Instead he saw a pair of dancing topaz eyes and bouncing copper ringlets.

"Jenny," he whispered the name almost reverently.

Why could he not get past her? Why did she haunt his dreams at night and his thoughts during the day? It had been almost six years since he last saw her and still the pain was almost physical.

They had only been kids, but the love he felt for her was as real now as it had been then.

The same old questions threatened to resurface, but he forced them back down. It wouldn't do any good anyway. Her disappearance was just as much of a mystery to him now as it had been the day he'd realized she was gone.

The last day of school Trevor had skipped class and rode out to the McGreggor farm to confront the frizzy, orange headed woman and the bald man, whom he learned was Jenny's Aunt and Uncle. It took two weeks of hounding them every day before they finally admitted that she'd run away the night after he had gone looking for her. Neither seemed to know where she'd gone, and Trevor got the distinct impression that they didn't care either.

At only fifteen he'd been too young to go after her himself, but he'd tried anyway. He'd only made it as far as Oak Springs when his father and brother had caught up to him. His father had been furious and his brother had teased him unmercifully.

Trevor had been devastated, and although his family loved him, no one noticed since his sister Katie disappeared only a few days later. With each one in their own grief no one knew about Trevor's turmoil. Everyone just assumed he was upset over Katie too, which was partly true. But for Trevor the pain was doubled.

It wasn't until he came to know the Lord about a year later that the healing was able to start and he was able to put both Jenny and Katie in His capable hands.

Trevor smiled as he thought about his sister and her family. She had been back for a little over a year now and had married their brother, Luke's best friend. He had always had a fondness for Lance and it just felt right for him to be an actual part of their family now.

He was truly thankful for the miracle God had wrought when He brought Katie back to them, and he knew that if God willed it He could bring Jenny back to him too.

Trevor sent up another little prayer as he threw off his quilt and shivered as his feet hit the cold floor. It was still unusually cold for late April, but by noon it would be absolutely perfect weather for their Easter picnic.

"Thank you Lord for the hope you rose from the dead to give us," he prayed as he knelt by his bed and tears began to make their way down his cheeks. "Thank you for the awesome sacrifice you made for such a wretch as me. I sure love you and I wish only to serve you. Thank you for the call you have placed on my life Lord. Please use me, make me, and mold me into the preacher you would have me to be, and Lord if it be Thy will, please bring Jenny back to me."

~*~*~*~

Jenny was exhausted by the time she made it to her room. Her eyes took in the spacious, richly furnished room and noted that Millie hadn't made it back to their room yet.

It had been a long night and her feet were killing her. She was glad of the dark, velvet, burgundy drapes gracing her windows. Not only were they beautiful, but they blocked out any light from the cheerful morning sun.

Jenny sighed to herself. She was a creature of the night. She couldn't remember the last time she'd enjoyed the mid-day sunshine.

She had been at this since her parents had died when she was only fourteen years old. All alone and on the streets she had never been so scared in her life. She knew the kind of life awaiting someone like her, but after over hearing a conversation between her Aunt Beatrice and Uncle Bert she knew she had no choice. She had heard what orphanages were like and there was no way she would allow them to send her to one.

Her mom had been a dance hall girl before she'd moved them to Riverview. It was an excellent living for a single woman and, more often than not, the only sort of work available besides prostitution. Something Jenny refused to do. She might look like a whore, but she was proud that she wasn't.

She had only been kissed by one man in her lifetime, if you could call him that. At only fifteen Trevor Rollins hadn't been a man full grown, but in many ways he was way more man than the poor wretches she danced with all night long.

Jenny sighed again, but this was a different kind of sigh as she remembered the one and only love she had ever experienced. She glanced down at the topaz ring that still graced her dainty finger. The only time she had taken it off was when she'd had to get it resized as she grew into womanhood.

She could still remember the feel of the metal as Trevor slid it onto her right, ring finger. She could still hear his laughter, see his smile and feel his lips on hers. She could still see the image he made as he rode out of her life for the last time. The day he left he took her heart with him and she'd left it there with him the night she ran away.

After running away she found herself in a good sized town called Oak Springs. Alone and on the streets she'd tried to avoid the inevitable, but no one wanted to hire her at the dinner, mercantile or anywhere else for that matter.

Then one night she was darting through the back alley ways when she heard the music and seemed drawn to the swinging doors of her own volition.

Horace had just pulled up in his coach looking so elegant and refined. He spotted her right away and wove a spell of charm around her as he promised her everything short of the moon.

Horace wasn't perfect, but he was very protective over his girls and didn't allow any foolishness. The same thing couldn't be said for the man that ran the Honky Tonk on the other side of town.

"Prostitution is bad business," Horace always said. "Too many risks involved."

He didn't put up with loose women either. He'd sent more than one girl packing to the other side of town, but to those of good moral character he was unerringly generous and kind. He expected them to earn their keep, but they were the best paid dancehall girls in all of Texas.

Jenny had just sat down at her dressing table when her roommate and best friend Millie walked in. There were four women in all that worked for Horace. The other two women Goldie and Lylla were more than ten years older than she was, but both women had hearts of gold and looked out for the younger girls. Millie was the only one her age and she had come to work for Horace only days after Jenny had. Millie's story was almost an exact replica of Jenny's, accept her mom was the only one that had died and Millie had to runaway to avoid the advances of her stepfather.

Their pasts alike and their fates intertwined, they had become more than just friends. Each one looked at the other as a sister and therefore the only family they each had.

"Oh girl, I'm exhausted," Millie exclaimed as she plopped down unceremoniously onto her bed.

"Me too," Jenny admitted. "No one is going to have to rock me to sleep today."

"Me either," Millie agreed. "I'm not sure I even want to take the time to dress for bed. I could just go ahead and curl up just like this."

"Oh, and you'll sleep just fine like that too," Jenny said sarcastically with a giggle as she picked up her horsehair brush. "In our line of work little baggies under our eyes simply won't do."

"You know I think you're crazy for ironing your hair every evening," Millie informed her as she watched her friend run the brush through her straitened copper locks. "I would kill to have those natural curls of yours."

Jenny gave an unlady like snort. "Trust me; your raven black, straight tresses are far more appealing than my unruly, red hair. Now the latter I can't do much about, but I can at least bring some order to the chaos."

"Curls aren't chaotic Jenny, and I would kill to have hair your hair color too," Millie argued as she to sat at her own dressing table and started pulling pins out of her hair.

"Okay, enough about my hair," Jenny said closing the subject. "How was your night?"

"Mostly the same," Millie answered as she stood up, crossed the room and stepped behind her dressing screen, "danced till I felt like my feet were going to fall off, tried to keep from being groped on and still entice the men enough to get them to the bar to buy a drink or two."

"I did pretty good on drink commissions tonight," Jenny admitted to her friend. "You know what doesn't make any sense to me Millie?"

"Oh, no," Millie laughed and sighed dramatically, "here we go again."

"What? You know I'm right," Jenny defended. "We convince them to go to the bar and drink, and then when they get drunk they step out of line with us and have to be escorted out. It's just a messed up system if you ask me."

"Well, Horace doesn't see it that way," Millie gave an unlady like snort. "All he cares about is getting his hands on their money, and as far as he's concerned by the time they've had enough to be drunk he's gotten his fair share of it anyway."

"And us too, I suppose," Jenny admitted, "but it just seems wrong somehow."

"Well, right or wrong, it seems to be the only thing we are cut out for," Millie said while climbing into her bed and snuggling under her covers.

"It's what we are cut out for now Millie, but what about when we get too old to be attractive?"

"To be honest Jenny, I try not to think about that," Millie admitted.

"I know it's not a pleasant subject, but the Bible says that our lives are like a vapor," Jenny replied climbing beneath her own covers, "doesn't sound like they last very long to me."

"Jenny Lynn McGreggor!" Millie exclaimed sitting up in bed to stare at her friend. "How would you know what the Bible says?!"

Jenny sat up and shrugged her shoulders. "After my momma married my dad we started going to church," tears filled Jenny's eyes as she remembered her best memories. "I loved attending church," she admitted.

"I used to go to church with my momma too," Millie admitted, her eyes also growing moist.

"I didn't know that," Jenny said in wonder.

"I didn't know about you either," Millie countered.

"I guess I just don't...well I don't feel worthy anymore," Jenny told her friend. "I never quite understood it anyway and speaking about God or the Bible after what I've become just seems hypocritical."

"Yah," Millie agreed, "I feel the same way, but sometimes I still pray."

"You do?" Jenny asked in surprise.

"I pray and ask God to remove us both from this situation," Millie admitted, "I don't believe this is what he had in mind when he created us."

"Me neither," Jenny agreed. "Do you think he will listen to a couple of saloon girls?"

"My momma used to say that he loved the whole world," Millie smiled at Jenny. "I suppose that means us too."

"I never thought about it that way," Jenny admitted, "Him loving us I mean, but I do recall my Daddy reading something about it out of his Bible one time."

"Well then, if the Bible said it I recon it's true," Millie replied, "and if he loves us then I don't recon it can hurt to pray."

"How will I know if He's listening or not?" Jenny asked.

"Not sure about that," Millie admitted as she snuggled back underneath her covers. "But like I said, it can't hurt."

"I guess not," Jenny conceded as she also snuggled beneath her covers. "Good night Millie."

"Good night Jenny."

Chapter 2

Colorful quilts dotted the church's lawn. Three of them belonged to his family. One for his brother Luke's family, one for his sister Katie's family and one for his parents, Seth and Ruby, and him.

Trevor watched as his little nieces and nephew crawled back and forth between everyone's picnics. Aisley, Luke and LeAnn's daughter, was just starting to walk, but preferred to crawl with her cousins when they were together. She was a beautiful child with jet black hair and dancing violet eyes like her mother. Her cheeks were rosy against her cream complexion.

Katie and Lance's plump twins were just as beautiful with their Indian inherited, dark complexions and sporting some healthy, rosy cheeks of their own. Blake's eyes were like his mothers, green as spring grass. While Brooke's were like her father's, blue as the brightest sky.

"Trevor, I think Hillary was disappointed you didn't ask her to sit with us today," Luke teased.

"No," Lance chimed in, "I thought it was Amy, or was it Marcy?"

"All right you two," Ruby said sending them both a mock glare, "leave me baby alone."

"It was Marcy," Luke continued teasing, "or was it Nancy?"

"No, it was definitely Amy," Lance chuckled.

"I thought it was Ms. Harrison," Trevor teased back.

"Oh!" Luke laughed, "So that's the way the wind blows?"

"He doesn't want one of those young girls," Lance laughed along with Luke and Trevor. "He wants someone like Widow Harrison with more experience!"

"Boys!" Ruby exclaimed in exasperation. "They'll hear you! Seth, do something!"

"Now boys," Seth tried to sound stern, but he was struggling not to laugh himself.

"Sorry Momma," they said in unison, but couldn't stop laughing.

"Seriously Trevor," Katie spoke up while playfully smacking her husband on the arm, "when are you going to try to settle down?"

"Maybe never," Trevor replied honestly and all laughter died.

"What do you mean never?" LeAnn asked her brother-in-law.

"I just mean that if God doesn't send me the right one then...well," Trevor shrugged his shoulders, "it may be never."

"Son, a man needs a helpmate by his side," his dad broke into the conversation. "God said it wasn't good for man to be alone."

"I'm not alone," Trevor smiled reassuringly at them all, "I have all of you."

"Yes you do, but that's not what I meant son," Seth answered.

"I know what you meant Dad, but..." Trevor hadn't spoken of Jenny to anyone since the day Katie left. He knew they had all forgotten her, and he wasn't sure he was ready to remind them about her. It would be like pouring salt on an open wound.

"But what Baby?" Ruby asked patting his hand in a show of support

"But it's just not time," Trevor finished lamely. "I'll keep a look out though, and when or if God does put my special someone in my path I'll know it."

"That's all we can ask for," Ruby said sending everyone a look that said this conversation was closed.

Aside from the awkward conversation, Trevor had a great time at the picnic. The men had played horseshoes; the women had set up quilting in the church, while the kids played various games in the yard. It was getting close to evening time when everyone started packing up.

"Trevor, I want you to take these leftovers home," his mother informed him. "Why don't you place them in the wagon and then we'll run them over to your place before heading to the farm."

"You can have ours too," LeAnn chimed in.

"Ours too," Katie said already taking a covered dish to her parents' wagon.

"Have I ever told you ladies how much I love our church socials?" Trevor teased as he climbed into the wagon bed and the women started handing him food. "Or rather, the leftover food from our church socials?"

"Why don't we go ahead and take these on over to your house?" Ruby asked after they had the wagon all loaded up. "Your father is in a meeting with the pastor and the other deacons."

"Okay Momma," Trevor said as he leapt from the wagon bed and helped her into the front seat.

As he drove the wagon down Main Street Trevor glanced around at his home town. He loved Riverview. There wasn't much to it, just red clay and sage brush, but it was home. To most people it probably seemed like a plain town, but Trevor loved the familiarity and the town's view of the wide Red River to the south.

Shops lined the boardwalk of the small Texas town on both sides of Main Street. Not much had changed in Riverview since Trevor was a boy and he found himself trying to see what it would look like through Jenny's eyes if she were there.

Thompson's Mercantile, the town bank, the Riverview Bed and Breakfast, and the same old, dilapidated jail all sat on one side of the red clay street and on the other side sat an empty office where Dr. McKinney use to be. Next were Pop's Barber Shop, and Mr. Allen's Smithy and Livery. A red school house with black trim was the town's only new addition.

Trevor couldn't bear to see the old schoolhouse torn down, and with it his memories, so he'd purchased the building, remodeled it and made it a small cottage.

The ride from the church at the end of town to Trevor's little cottage didn't take long. He used to live in the apartment behind the Livery, but with him being such a big man, he found he needed more space and the newly converted cottage turned out to be just what he needed.

At eighteen Trevor had moved to town to begin apprenticing under Mr. Allen the blacksmith. Trevor loved blacksmithing and he was a little sad he wouldn't be using the trade he'd worked so hard to learn, but he was honored to have been called into the ministry and knew he wouldn't be truly happy doing anything else; not even blacksmithing. The call to preach the Word of God was a burning desire unlike anything else he'd ever experienced.

"Trevor," his mother was the first to break the companionable silence.

"Yes Ma'am," he answered

"I'm sorry I haven't been a very good mother to you," she shocked him by saying as her eyes filled with tears.

"What?" Trevor didn't have a clue what she was talking about as far as he was concerned there wasn't a better mother in the whole world. "Mom you're the best…."

Ruby raised a hand to silence him. "No Son, I'm not fishing for compliments. I have been so wrapped up in my own grief that I didn't see yours." Ruby's voice cracked as she fought back her tears, "Not until today."

"Mom, I'm fine," Trevor tried to assure her, but she just shook her head.

"No Son," she denied. "You're not fine. I don't know how a mother, someone who's supposed to put you above anything and anyone could have been so blind, and I'm so very sorry." Ruby couldn't hold back any longer as one sob escaped and then another.

Trevor hated to see his mother cry above all else and pulled her into his arms.

"It's alright Momma," he soothed. He didn't know what all of this was about, but nothing was worth this. "Please don't cry."

~ 35 ~

"It's right that I should cry," Ruby defended. "How many times have you cried Son? How many times have you suffered alone? You were so young I thought it was just a crush. I had no idea you have loved her all these years."

Trevor couldn't seem to draw breath into his lungs. She was right. He had cried and suffered alone, but he'd never blamed his family for it.

"I don't even remember her name," his mother wailed.

"Jenny," he whispered. Ruby sat back and stared at him in wonder. "Her name was Jenny."

"Jenny," his mother slowly nodded her head and smiled. "Yes, I remember now. Her hair always reminded me of a shiny new penny."

"Me too," Trevor agreed his voice thick with emotion. "Her eyes always reminded me of that stone," Trevor said pointing to the ring on his mother's right hand.

"How can you ever forgive me?" Ruby asked.

"There's nothing to forgive Momma," Trevor answered truthfully.

"Yes there is Son and somehow I'll make it up to you," Ruby told him as she placed a soft hand on his cheek, "and I'm going to start with this," she said as she slid the ring from her finger and placed it in his hand.

"I can't accept this Momma," Trevor argued as he tried to give it back to her.

"You can, and you will Son," Ruby informed him as she folded her arms in a show of stubbornness. "I am praying that one day you can give it to her."

"But what if I never see her again?" Trevor asked still holding out the ring.

"You will Baby," Ruby told him without a trace of doubt. "I know it as sure as I breathe. Did she love you?"

"Yes Ma'am," Trevor replied with certainty.

"Then she'll come back to you," Ruby smiled at him. "Love always finds a way."

"Thank you Momma," Trevor said as he leaned down and placed a kiss on her cheek. "I love you."

"I love you too Sweetheart," Ruby replied while praying that the Father would bring Jenny back swiftly.

~*~*~*~

Jenny stepped off the train and onto the Riverview platform. Her pulse raced as she spotted him. He was taller than she remembered, but she would know him anywhere.

"Trevor," she yelled and waved.

"Jenny?" Trevor asked in wonder.

"Yes Trevor," she laughed as tears filled her eyes, "it's me. I'm so sorry I left you."

"Oh Jenny!" Trevor exclaimed as he raced forward, grabbed her around the waist and spun her around. "You came back to me!"

"And I'm never leaving you again," Jenny promised.

Then as if in a trance they moved forward in unison. Jenny could almost feels his breath on her lips and knew he was about to kiss her.

"Jenny...Jenny...,"

Her face made a frown as a very feminine voice intruded on this special moment that she had waited for, for so long.

"Jenny…It's time to wake up."

Jenny blinked at her best friend and then buried her head under her pillows. With any luck she could return to her dream and receive the kiss that she'd been waiting over five years and hundreds of dreams for.

"Jenny you promised we could go dress shopping today," Millie giggled, "and who the heck is Trevor anyway?"

That got Jenny's attention as she bolted up in bed smacking Millie's forehead with her own in the process.

"Owwww," Millie laughed while grabbing her throbbing head.

"Ohhhh!" Jenny exclaimed grabbing her own. "Sorry about that."

"No need to get violent," Millie teased. "It was just a question."

Jenny laughed, "That's what you get for interrupting people's best dreams and asking nosey questions."

"Fair enough," Millie conceded, "but you did tell me to wake you up when I got up so we could go shopping."

"Oh alright," Jenny teased with a dramatic sigh that would have done any actress proud.

~*~*~*~

Oak Springs was bustling with activity. Aside from the occasional snide remark from the "genteel ladies" of the town, and some lewd gestures from a couple men, it was a glorious Monday afternoon as they strolled past various shops and other businesses.

On one side of the street there was a large single story bank, Bradley's Mercantile, Nip & Tuck seamstress shop, and a fairly new jail. On the other side there was the Oak Springs Boarding House, a restaurant called Pearl's Place, Butler's Barber Shop, and Horace's Place where they lived. A Dr. B. Michael's office sat beside the saloon and on the other side of that sat the Lonestar Hotel. A pretty little white church, with pink, flowering azalea bushes in front sat at the end of Main Street as if it was overseeing the town. There were roads branching off of the main street that led to quaint neighborhoods and more businesses such as Mason's Drug Store, a white washed clapboard school house with red trim, Taylor Meat Market, Grandma's Bakery, Smith's Livery, the town hall, and a second saloon that just read Honky-Tonk.

It was a fairly large town, but everyone still knew who, or better yet, what they were in spite of their common clothing. The best friends kept their heads high and chatted back and forth as they headed for their favorite seamstress.

They were just passing Pearl's Place when they encountered a couple of rough looking characters. Both men were huge and filthy. They let out low whistles as the women walked by. They tried to ignore them until one of the men reached out and patted Millie's bottom.

Millie let out a shriek and both men started laughing.

~ 39 ~

"Do NOT touch her," Jenny spat as her eyes shot topaz fire.

"Would you rather we touch you?" the other man crooned as he reached out and grabbed a fistful of the curls Millie had begged her not to iron.

"I would not!" Jenny screamed as her knee connected with his groin. She felt a great sense of satisfaction when he doubled over and dropped to the ground, writhing in pain.

"Why you little…"

"What seems to be the trouble here?" A sharply dressed, handsome man carrying a Dr.'s bag interrupted.

"None of your business," the man still standing growled. "Best if you carry on and leave the ladies to us."

"I don't think so," the handsome man said while pulling a .45 seemingly out of nowhere. "I think you and your buddy here are going to be doing the leaving."

"Don't," the man on the ground shouted as his buddy took a foolish step forward. "They're not worth it."

"But Travis…"

"I said no Jonas," the injured man said staggering to his feet. "I don't aim to lose my only cousin today. Come on, we'll find us a couple of whores to wrestle with"

"Excuse me, but I'd appreciate it if you'd refrain from that kind of talk around the ladies," Mr. Tall, dark and handsome said drawing the hammer back on his .45.

"Whatever you say mister," the man named Travis said as he tipped his hat to the ladies sarcastically, and shoved the man he'd called Jonas, down the boardwalk.

After the men were out of earshot their rescuer turned toward them.

"Hello," he greeted with a smile. "I'm Dr. Blain Michaels."

"Hi Dr. Michaels, I'm Jenny McGreggor and this is my friend Millicent Reynolds," Jenny and Millie beamed at him.

"Thank you so much for your help," Millie blushed, "Dr. Michaels."

"Yes thank you," Jenny agreed.

"You ladies are more than welcome," Dr. Michaels addressed them both, but his gaze never left Millie. "May I escort you to wherever it is that you are going?"

"Oh, that really isn't…"

"I insist," Dr. Michaels interrupted Jenny's refusal. "It's not every day I get to escort such lovely ladies."

Jenny had to fight to keep from rolling her eyes as Millie giggled and the Dr. offered her his arm. This was not going to end well!

~*~*~*~

Blain couldn't believe his good fortune! He had been trying to find a way to introduce himself to the raven haired beauty on his arm since he first spotted her crossing the street months ago.

He had tried to ask around about her discreetly, but no one knew of a lady that fit his description, and he hadn't even used the words he really thought that described the angel on his arm! He simply had to find out more about

~ 41 ~

her. How could he court her if he didn't even know where she lived?

"I've seen you ladies around town before," he hoped his voice sounded nonchalant. "Do you live here in town?"

"We live at the..."

"Yes, we live here in town," Millie rushed in cutting off her friend.

"Really? Where abouts?" Blain asked.

"Oh look!" Millie exclaimed as they reached the Nip and Tuck. "This is our destination. Thank you so much for your assistance. Come Jenny," she said grabbing the redhead's hand and practically pulling her toward the shop's entrance, "we're here."

"Yes, I can see that Millie," Jenny giggled. "Have a good day Dr. Michaels."

With that, both women disappeared into the shop, leaving a bewildered doctor in their wake.

~*~*~*~

"What was that?" Jenny asked her best friend.

"What was what?" Millie asked innocently.

"Oh! You know very well what Millicent Ruth Reynolds!" Jenny scolded.

"Oh, I don't know Jenny Lynn McGreggor," Millie snapped. "Maybe it was nice for a decent man to pay me attention for a change, and just maybe I didn't want that decent man to know who, or better yet, what I am."

"Oh, Millie," Jenny sighed, "I'm sorry. I just don't want you hurt, but I do understand."

"I know," Millie sighed too. "I won't get hurt, but it will be nice to look back on today and remember that a good man thought I was a lady."

"A handsome, good man too," Jenny teased waggling her brows at her friend.

"That he was," Millie giggled and then sighed dreamily. "Have you ever seen a more handsome man?"

"Well..."

"Scratch that," Millie raised one finely arched brow, "I'm sure he doesn't compare to the elusive Trevor I hear you dreaming about."

"Millie!"

"What?!" Millie laughed. "It's true isn't it?"

"Why have you never told me I talk in my sleep?" Jenny felt her face go hot.

"Would it have made a difference?" Millie teased.

"Yes, I would have gagged and taped my own mouth shut every night before I went to bed!" Jenny laughed.

"What on earth is going on out here?"

Both women immediately stopped laughing as they watched the beautiful brunet seamstress emerge from the backroom.

"We're sorry Elizabeth," Jenny apologized, "I know we normally come in the back way, but we had someone escort us here today and Millie didn't want him to see us going in the back and ask questions."

"Him?" Elizabeth eyed them suspiciously. "Anyone I know?"

"I recon the whole town should know who he is since he's the…"

"Jenny, would you please be quite!" Millie hissed.

"Oh, pish posh Millie! It's just me," Elizabeth giggled. "You can tell me."

"It was Dr. Michaels," Jenny rushed on before Millie could stop her.

"Blain?!" Elizabeth asked as her amber eyes widened in surprise. "He's Eric's best friend."

"Oh Jenny, why couldn't you have just keep it between us?" Millie scolded.

"It's just Elizabeth, Millie," Jenny tried to reason with her friend, "she isn't going to tell him who we are. Are you Elizabeth?"

"Of course not," Elizabeth assured her friend. "But I must admit it all makes sense now."

"What makes sense?" Millie asked as her brows knit in confusion.

"Oh…I'm not sure I should say," the seamstress teased as she casually turned and went back to the backroom.

"Oh no you don't Elizabeth Chandler!" Jenny laughed as both friends trailed behind her. "What do you know about Dr. Michaels?"

"Well…" Elizabeth looked around conspiratorially, "I know that he has been asking around about a beautiful, black haired, blue eyed woman that he happened to see crossing the street a few months back."

Jenny's jaw dropped while Millie squealed.

"He's been searching for me Jenny!" Millie laughed as she spun around. "He thinks I'm beautiful!"

"Now wait a minute Millie," Jenny didn't want to hurt her friend, but facts were facts and what Millie needed right now was a good reminder of the cold hard facts. "We aren't even sure if it is you he's looking for."

"But she's the only one..." Elizabeth was silenced as Jenny raised her hand to hold off the arguments that were sure in coming.

"Even if it is you he's looking for, when he finds out your occupation all the interest he has in you will fly out the window. Upstanding members of the community like Dr. Michaels don't go around marrying dancehall girls. If he still wants to have something to do with you after he finds out what you are, it won't be marriage on his mind," Jenny hated herself as she watched the tears fill her friend's eyes.

"Now wait just one hairy minute Jenny Lynn McGreggor!" Elizabeth huffed as she wrapped an arm around Millie's shoulders. "Blain Michaels is a fine Christian man. If he shows interest in Millie it won't be for anything less than marriage."

"Then either God will perform a miracle, or he won't want to have anything to do with her at all," Jenny gave them both a sheepish smile. "But for your sake, my sweet Millie, I pray God performs a miracle."

"He is in the miracle working business," Elizabeth exclaimed, "and since when do you two start talking about God anyway?"

"Please don't think us hypocritical Elizabeth, but we are praying that God will intervene in our lives," Millie said shyly.

"That's right," Jenny agreed, "We want real lives with families of our own."

Elizabeth's heart broke for her friends. No one in town knew these two women like she did. No one took the time. All they seen were dancehall girls, but when they had shyly approached her a few years back asking for some respectable clothes to go out in public with, Elizabeth couldn't deny them. They had become fast friends. They insisted that they should enter through the back of the shop, and that she should keep their friendship a secret for her sake, but Elizabeth wouldn't have cared who knew.

After she'd married her husband, Eric, had put up a fuss, but she had insisted that he get to know them before he cast judgment. After meeting them in the shop a few times he had agreed that she should continue her friendship with them.

"I will pray for it too," Elizabeth assured them as tears filled her eyes and spilled onto her cheeks. She couldn't resist pulling each woman into her arms for a quick embrace. "The Bible says in Matthew 18:19 "That if two of you shall agree on earth as touching anything that they shall ask, it shall be done for them of my Father which is in heaven."

"It says that?" they both said in unison.

"Yes it does," Elizabeth assured them with a wink. "The way I see it if you two agree and me and Eric agree together for the same thing it's bound to get God's attention."

"I hope so," Jenny smiled.

"Me too," Millie agreed.

"You can't hope ladies," Elizabeth warned and both of them looked at her in confusion. "You have to have faith that he will do what you are asking. Do you believe the Bible is true?"

"Of course," they said.

"Well the Bible said if you agreed together he would do anything you asked, so now all you have to do is have faith," Elizabeth clarified. "The Word of God teaches us that faith is the only thing that pleases God and without it it's impossible."

"Then we're gonna have faith. Right Millie?" Jenny said linking her arms with each of her friends'.

"Right," Millie agreed

~*~*~*~

Blain decided that an early dinner was in order and just "happened" to sit at a table that had a perfect view to all the shops across the street. He discreetly tried to keep a constant vigil on Elizabeth's shop which was why he knew the moment the two women left. Part of him wanted to follow them, but he didn't want them to think he was a weirdo, so instead he decided to do the next best thing and interrogate his best friend's wife.

"Why, hello Blain," Elizabeth called cheerfully as she emerged from the back room. "I'm afraid Eric isn't here yet."

"I'm not here to see Eric," Blain admitted as a blush stained his cheeks. Maybe this wasn't such a good idea.

"Oh, I thought you just bought a new wardrobe," Elizabeth said nonchalantly as she absently brushed at one of the mannequins in the shop window. "Did something not fit right?"

"No, no everything was perfect," Blain rushed to assure her.

"Did you decide you needed something else?" Elizabeth asked as she continued to fuss with the mannequin.

"No...Yes! I need...I need," Blain wracked his brain for an excuse to be there, "I need..."

"A wife?" Elizabeth offered as though he were only needing another shirt.

"Yes...No! I mean..." Blain stuttered to a stop as Elizabeth burst out laughing. "How did you know?"

"Come now Blain," Elizabeth tease, "You've been asking around about a beautiful black haired, blue eyed woman for weeks, and Millie just exited my shop. I do believe she fits your description."

"Well I," Blain rubbed the back of his neck in a bashful gesture, "I was hoping you could tell me more about her," he admitted.

"I'll be happy to tell you what I can," Elizabeth assured him then turned serious. "All I ask is that you don't cast judgment until you've heard me out."

"Why would I cast judgment on you?" Blain asked in confusion.

"It's not me I'm worried about," she admitted as she chewed on her lower lip. "Look Blain, Millie and Jenny are very dear to me. They are good, decent women, but most of the town's people have never taken the time to get to know them."

"Why ever not?" he asked in confusion.

"Because they are…because they work at Horace's Place," Elizabeth sighed. This would be a test for the young doctor's character for sure. Not many "Christians" could over look her friends' profession.

"You mean they're prostitutes?" Blain asked incredulously.

"NO!" Elizabeth denied vehemently. "They are NOT prostitutes. They are merely dancehall girls. All they do is dance."

"Oh, that's good," Blain said sounding relieved. "I mean that's not good, but it's better than the alternative."

"I agree, and so do they," Elizabeth surprised him by saying.

"They don't like their profession?" Blain asked hoping it was so.

"No, they do not," Elizabeth informed him. "As a matter of fact they are both praying that God will provide a way for them to leave the dancehall behind. They want normal lives with homes, husbands and babies of their own."

"You know I've never had a woman affect me the way Millie does," Blain admitted. "One look was all it took for me to be hooked."

"So I noticed," Elizabeth giggled.

"I do believe that she is the woman God made for me," Blain shocked Elizabeth by saying.

"But you don't even know her!" Elizabeth exclaimed.

"I will," he informed her.

"Now hold on Blain," Elizabeth warned as she placed a hand on his arm. "I know what you're thinking, but you are going to catch a lot of flack if you start courting one of Horace's girls."

"I don't care," Blain told her and meant it. "Mille is going to be my wife, and you are going to help me make it happen."

"How am I going to do that?" Elizabeth asked.

"You are going to tell me everything you know about her," Blain gave her a conspiratorial wink, "and it wouldn't hurt to set up some "accidental" rendezvous."

"Okay," Elizabeth laughed, "count me in!" She had always had a lot of respect for the doctor, but he had just lifted himself to knight in shining armor status as far as she was concerned and that was exactly what her friend deserved.

Chapter 3

Jenny felt a little naked as she descended the saloon stairs four days later. After wearing a modest, comfortable calico dress all afternoon it irked her to have to don her working dress. The red silk and black lace creation was her least favorite anyway, but at least it was slightly longer than her other ones. Most of her dresses landed just below her knees, but this one at least covered her calves, even if it did still show her ankles.

The neckline was low and the bodice snug. The corset was cinched up painfully tight; pressing her ample bosom together to form deep cleavage. Millie was always teasing her that she got bigger tips because of her bigger bust.

Before reaching the bottom step Jenny had already spotted Millie on the dance floor in her royal blue silk. Like herself she was painted up to look the part. Jenny had always thought it sad that someone so beautiful had to cover it up with paint.

She was greeted by the usual patrons and was asked to dance before her booted foot left the last step.

The first half of the evening was Friday night, business as usual. Fridays were Jenny's least favorite nights. It seemed as though every cowpoke for miles around made it into the saloon on Friday nights. By the time the night was over Jenny would have a hard time standing, let alone dancing.

The late night hour was well underway when two familiar shadows pushed through the swinging doors, and

Jenny groaned inwardly. The man she was sitting at the counter with was already three shades to the wind, so she politely excused herself after downing the last of her tea to find Millie.

Jenny spotted her best friend at a black jack table and motioned for her. She watched as Millie excused herself and headed her way.

"What's up?" Millie asked as she reached Jenny's side.

"You remember those two men that accosted us on the street Monday?"

"The ones that Mr. Tall, dark and handsome took care of?" Millie asked as she sighed dreamily. Jenny didn't even bother to remind her that she had already started taking care of one of them before Dr. Michaels showed up.

"Yes," Jenny laughed.

"What about them?"

"They just walked into the saloon," Jenny told her nodding toward where the giants were sitting.

"Oh no! Really?" Millie exclaimed. "Couldn't they have just gone to the Honky Tonk?"

"I guess not," Jenny sighed. "Just be careful alright."

"I will," Millie promised, "You watch your back too."

"Don't I always?" Jenny teased, but her smile died as she locked eyes with the man called Travis. She had hoped they wouldn't recognize them, but the shocked expression on his face said he knew exactly who she was. She wasn't afraid; not really, she knew that Horace wouldn't allow any funny business, and as big as they were, Jimmy, the bouncer, was bigger.

"They've spotted us," she warned just as Millie started to head back to the black jack table.

"What?" Millie asked as she watched the men stand up and make their way toward them. "Oh my! What are we gonna do?"

"We are going to treat them like any other man in this bar," Jenny informed her as she raised her chin in defiance. "We're going to dance with them if they ask, and try to talk them into buy a drink at the bar. Their money is just as good as any other."

"Right," Millie agreed as she too raised her chin at the newcomers.

"Well, well," Travis whistled low, "looky what we have here Jonas! Aren't these the same "respectable" ladies we encountered on the street earlier this week?"

"Why I do believe it is," Jonas agreed as his eyes greedily devoured Millie.

"What a pleasant surprise this is," Travis chuckled as he sidled up to Jenny. "What do you say Darlin? Do you wanna dance?"

"Sure," Jenny agreed noting that his eyes never left her chest, "if you've got the money. I've got the time."

"What about you Pretty Lady?" Jenny heard Jonas ask Millie, but Travis was already whisking her onto the dance floor, so she didn't get to hear Millie's response, but when she and Jonas joined them on the dance floor Jenny got her answer.

"I can't tell you how excited I am to find you here tonight," Travis crooned. "I have been able to get you off my mind even once this week."

"I'm flattered," Jenny said sarcastically.

"You should be," Travis told her finally looking into her eyes. Jenny was appalled at the raw lust she saw burning there. "There's only been one other woman to occupy my thoughts so completely. I had her, and I'll have you too."

"Sorry to disappoint you Mr...?"

"No need to stand on formalities Darlin," Travis chuckled. "You and I are about to get close," he pulled her tight against him, "real close."

"No, we aren't," Jenny informed him as she tried to push him away. "This is a dancehall only. If you want that kind of attention you'll have to visit the Honky Tonk."

"Done been there Darlin," Travis shocked her by saying. "Oh don't worry," he crooned, "none of them can hold a candle to you."

"Is there a problem here gentlemen?" a booming, masculine voice asked, and Jenny was relieved to see Horace standing behind them. She looked over and noticed that Millie too was trying to push her dance partner away.

"Who do you think you are?" Travis snarled.

"I'm Horace," her boss informed him with deadly calm.

"Is that supposed to mean something to us?" Jonas laughed sarcastically.

"This is my place, and those are my girls," Horace's eyes narrowed as he sized each man up. "If you can't treat them with respect you can leave."

"Relax Mr." Travis chuckled. "We're willing to pay for a few hours alone with your whores."

"These girls aren't whores, and there ain't enough money in all of Texas," Horace informed him. "Jimmy! Show these men the door."

The goliath bouncer seemed to appear out of nowhere as he grabbed both men by their collars and Jenny breathed a sigh of relief as he unceremoniously ushered them out of the saloon.

"Thanks Horace," Millie told him.

"Yah, thanks," Jenny agreed.

"I want to talk to both of you girls in the morning," Horace informed them.

"Yes sir," they said in unison before returning to work.

~*~*~*~

A new day was beginning to dawn by the time the last patron left the saloon, and Jenny plopped herself down onto a chair beside Millie.

"I'm ready for bed," Millie yawned.

"Me too," Jenny agreed with a yawn of her own, "but Mr. Bossy wants to see us before we head up for bed."

"Mr. Bossy is just concerned for your safety." Both women jumped at the sound of Horace's voice as he made his way to their table and took a seat of his own.

"Sorry Horace," Jenny apologized.

"No need to apologize Jenny," he chuckled, "I am perfectly aware of how grouchy you can get when you're tired."

"I do not get grouchy!" Jenny defended and glared at Millie when she giggled.

"Tell her I'm right Millie," Horace said with a smug smile.

"I refuse to answer on the grounds that it might incriminate me," Millie informed him but her eyes still twinkled with suppressed laughter.

"Chicken," Horace teased.

"Hey you're not the one that has to live with her!" Millie laughed.

"Alright you two," Jenny interrupted with a mock glare at them both, "if you don't get this meeting over with soon I'm going take my grouchy self to bed!"

"Fair enough," Horace chuckled. "I wanted to talk to you about those two men that Jimmy escorted out last night. What do you know about them?"

"Not much," Jenny answered honestly, "last night was only the second time we laid eyes on them."

"The second time," Horace drew his brows down, "When was the first?"

"Monday when we went out they accosted us on the street," Jenny informed him.

"But Dr. *Michaels* came to our defense," Millie sighed.

The way Millie had said Dr. Michaels' name wasn't lost on Horace. "How do you know Dr. Michaels?"

"We don't," Jenny informed him while sending Millie a warning glance. "Those men tried to assault us and Dr. Michaels stepped in."

"Hum," Horace said clearly not convinced. "Well, anyway I wanted to warn you about those men. They have been causing all kinds of trouble at the Honky Tonk.

~ 56 ~

Harry had one of his boys head over to warn me about them after they roughed up one of his girls."

Both women gasped in unison.

"Now I don't want to frighten you, but I do want you to be aware," Horace assured them.

"Thanks Horace," Millie told him.

"Is the girl going to be okay?" Jenny asked.

"I don't know," Horace answered honestly. "I hope so."

"Me too," Jenny said thinking of one of Harry's girls she'd run into a few weeks back. Darby was so young and it had broken Jenny's heart to learn that the sweet sixteen year old worked at the Honky Tonk. If it hadn't been for Horace finding her first who knows, she could have ended up like Darby.

~*~*~*~

It was a beautiful day as Jenny stepped out onto the boardwalk. Oak Springs was bustling with activity and Jenny was excited to be out in the sunshine as she headed toward the Nip and Tuck alone. Women smiled at her and nodded politely while men tipped their hats toward her respectfully.

She had almost reached Elizabeth's shop when she heard his voice.

"Jenny?" he asked in astonishment. "Jenny Lynn McGreggor?"

Her breath caught as she turned and saw the handsome man walking swiftly toward her. She would have known him anywhere.

"Trevor," Jenny breathed his name reverently.

"After all these years...I can't believe I've finally found you," He said in wonder.

"You've been looking for me?" Jenny asked in amazement.

"Of course I've been looking for you. Where have you been?" he asked.

"Oh Trevor," Jenny sighed as tears filled her eyes, "I'm so sorry, but I had to leave. They were going to send me to an orphanage."

"Shhh...Don't cry Jenny," Trevor soothed as he gathered her in his arms. "We're together now and it's going to be alright."

"I love you so much," Jenny confessed as she looked up into his handsome face.

"I love you too Sweetheart," Trevor whispered as he leaned forward ever so slowly. Jenny could almost feel his warm breath on her lips. "Jenny...Jenny...Jenny..."

Jenny's brow scrunched in frustration as Millie's voice intruded and Trevor vanished.

"Oh Millie!" Jenny wailed as she buried her head under her pillows.

"I know you'd rather stay in dreamland with the mysterious Trevor, but if we don't go now there won't be time to get our new dresses from Elizabeth before we have to start work," Millie giggled then burst out laughing when her best friend hurled a pillow at her.

"Oh, you sure are a party pooper," Jenny laughed as she sat up in bed and blink sleepily at her friend.

"Jenny," Millie said hesitantly, "who is Trevor. I know he must be special and you've never mentioned him accept in your sleep."

Jenny wasn't sure she wanted to sully her memories of Trevor by talking about him in a saloon, but Millie was her best friend and he was the only part of her world that she hadn't shared with her.

"The love of my life," Jenny said it so softly that Millie wasn't sure she'd heard her.

"But I don't know anyone named Trevor," Millie said as she drew her brows together in concentration and her mind started ticking off the men they had met.

"You've never met him," Jenny informed her. "Trevor was a part of my life before I moved to Oak Springs."

"But Jenny, you were only fourteen when you came here," Millie said incredulously.

"Yes, I was," Jenny agreed.

"And you met the love of your life at fourteen years old?" Millie asked clearly doubting it was possible to fall in love at fourteen.

"No," Jenny informed her and Millie started to relax, "I met him at seven years old."

"What?!" Millie exclaimed as her eyes threatened to swallow her face.

"The first day of school," Jenny laughed, and then proceeded to spill the entire love story out to Millie.

"Wow," Millie exclaimed in wonder once her friend had finished.

"I know," Jenny sighed. "It's a little hard for me to believe myself, but it's true."

"Oh, I believe you," Millie assured her. "It's just so sad. Do you think you'll ever see him again?"

"I don't know," Jenny admitted.

"You've just got to," Millie said adamantly.

"I'll tell you what we've got to do," Jenny said as she got up and made her way to her dressing table, "we've got to get dressed. If we waste anymore time there won't be any new dresses today."

"But I'm still not done talking about Trevor," Millie whined.

"Oh yes you are," Jenny laughed. "You woke me up for dresses and by George we are getting dresses."

"Party pooper," Millie teased as she too went about getting ready.

~*~*~*~

It was a beautiful spring day as the two friends stepped out onto the boardwalk. The walk to the Nip and Tuck didn't take long and before long they were knocking on the back door.

"Hello," Elizabeth said cheerfully as she let them in.

"Hello," they greeted in unison, then both women froze as they noticed that another person was present.

"Hello again ladies," Blain broke the silence. "It's a pleasure to see you both again."

"I see you have all met," Elizabeth said like she hadn't known.

"Yes," Blain replied as he smiled at Millie, "I had the pleasure of meeting them on Monday."

"It's good to see you again Dr. Michaels," Jenny told him sending Elizabeth a quizzical look, but when her friend wouldn't look her in the eye she was sure that something was up.

"Blain was just here for a fitting," Elizabeth informed them, but the blush creeping up her neck left room for doubt.

"Well we can just come back again tomorrow," Jenny offered.

"No!" three voices shouted in unison and Jenny busted out laughing.

"Jenny, could I talk to you for a minute?" Elizabeth asked already heading out of the back room.

Yep, something was definitely up and a talk with Elizabeth was exactly what she needed.

"Come on Millie," Jenny said grabbing Millie's arm and dragging her toward the door, "Elizabeth wants to talk to us."

"Actually…" Millie giggled while digging her feet in, "she just wanted to talk to you."

"Oh," Jenny said and sent Blain a suspicious look, but he only held up his hands and grinned unrepentantly. Jenny was not convinced. "Fine, but I'll be right back," she warned them both just before she sashayed off in search of Elizabeth.

~*~*~*~

"Hello," Blain said as he slowly approached Millie and stopped a respectable distance from her.

"Hello," Millie replied shyly.

"You know, I've been looking for you for a while now," Blain shocked her by admitting.

"Me?" she asked as she blushed to the roots of her hair. "Why?"

"Well," Blain chuckled, "because I saw you crossing the street and had never seen anyone so beautiful."

Millie could hardly breathe. She'd been told by many a man that she was beautiful, but this was different. This wasn't just some man at the saloon; this was a fine upstanding citizen of the community. This was a doctor, and she was a saloon girl. Suddenly reality hit her. This was no accident. Elizabeth had set this up, and Blain was about to declare an interest in her. It wouldn't work! She was no good for him.

"I have to go," she blurted out and tore out after Jenny leaving a bewildered Blain in her wake for the second time. Jenny was in a heated discussion with Elizabeth so Millie had no trouble finding her, grabbed her arm and pulled her out of the shop without even saying goodbye to Elizabeth.

"What happened?" Jenny asked sure that nothing so deplorable could have happened in the short amount of time they had been alone.

"You are right," Millie declared still dragging her friend toward Horace's Place. "There is no way it would work. What was I thinking?"

"Did he do something or say something to you?" Jenny asked ready to go back and confront him if he had stepped out of line with her friend.

"Yes!" Millie wailed. "He called me beautiful!"

~*~*~*~

"What happened?" Elizabeth asked.

"I don't know," Blain admitted. "All I did was tell her that I'd never seen anyone so beautiful before."

"And then what happened?"

"She told me she had to go and tore out of here with her friend in tow," Blain replied still running the scene through his mind for any clues as to what would have caused a reaction like that.

"I think she's just scared Blain," Elizabeth said gently. "Just give her some time."

"How much time?" Blain didn't have a clue how to go about courting Millie, but he knew he had to find a way.

"Just give her a few days and we'll try again," Elizabeth replied. "This time let me talk to them first. She needs to know more about you."

"What if she's just not interested in me?" Blain asked.

"Oh she's interested," Elizabeth assured him. "Trust me, she'll come around."

~*~*~*~

It had been another grueling night and Jenny was glad when break time rolled around. She desperately needed some fresh air, but she knew it wasn't safe to step onto the boardwalk, so she trudged up the stairs to her room and out onto her balcony. The air was chilly on Jenny's bare skin, but she didn't mind. She hated the stuffy, heated atmosphere of the saloon.

She looked forward to washing the stench of liquor, cigarettes and sweaty men off of her person.

Jenny noted that most of the town was dark. Not many people were up past midnight; not even on a Saturday night. A few of the men had even gone home, and she found herself wishing the rest would do the same. She hated her job. She hated the dresses, she hated the liquor and she hated the way the men made her feel, but what else could she do? Where could she go?

She closed her eyes and took a deep breath. She knew she needed to get back down stairs, but she couldn't bring herself to leave the semi quiet balcony.

When it was daylight she could see a pretty fair ways out of town from her balcony. She closed her eyes and pictured herself riding out of town and into the peaceful countryside. Somewhere where she didn't have to hear the plunking of the piano, or the carousing of the men. She longed to hear the crickets, and the frogs.

Jenny sighed and resigned herself to the inevitable. There would be no crickets or frogs to serenade her tonight; she had work to do.

She was just about to go back inside when she spotted them. They weren't really trying to hide in the shadows and Jenny felt a shiver run up her spine as she realized they had been watching her. She knew she was safe on the balcony, but she felt and urgent need to get to Millie and warn her.

Once back down stairs Jenny searched for Millie, but the only other females about were Goldie and Lylla, so she went to find Horace.

He wasn't hard to locate since he was almost always in the same spot.

"Horace," Jenny called as she reached the place where he stood by the piano, overseeing his domain. "Horace, I can't find Millie."

"I just sent her on break," her boss informed her.

"Did you see where she went?" Jenny asked

"No, I wasn't paying attention," Horace answered honestly.

"Those two men from last night are outside the saloon watching our balcony," Jenny rushed to tell him.

That got his attention. "Jimmy!" Horace bellowed for his bouncer

"Yah Boss," Jimmy's deep baritone rung out as he approached.

"Jimmy, those two fellas you threw out last night are lurking around outside," Horace informed him.

"I don't think there's much we can do about that Boss," Jimmy said shrugging his huge beefy shoulders.

"I know that!" Horace snapped, "I need to know if you've seen Millie?"

"I think she stepped outside for some fresh air just a few..."

"Onto the boardwalk?" Jenny interrupted as her heart started to pound and her feet started to move toward the door.

"Now hold on just one minute," Horace said as he grabbed her arm to stop her, "I don't want you out there."

"But…"

"No buts Jenny, I'll find Millie. Why don't you hold down the fort for me till I get back," he didn't wait for an answer, and Jenny watched helplessly as he disappeared through the crowd.

"Don't worry Jenny," Jimmy said as he followed after Horace, "I'll go with him. We'll find her."

Jenny tried to act like everything was alright, but as the minutes ticked by that got harder and harder. She was just about to reach panic mode when Horace reappeared at her side. The relief she felt was physical until she saw his grim expression.

"We can't find her," the words rung in her ears over and over again.

"What do you mean you can't find her," Jenny screeched. "You can't give up!"

"Sweetheart, I'm not giving up," Horace soothed, "I promise I'll find her, but first I have to clear everyone out of here…"

Jenny didn't waste any time as she climbed on top of the piano, pinched her tongue with her thumb and index finger and let out an ear piercing whistle that would have done her mother proud. That effectively grabbed the attention of every man and woman in the room.

"Alright everyone," Jenny yelled, "we have an emergency, so we need you all to leave. Now!" She added the last word when everyone just seemed to stare at her in confusion.

"Is she serious Horace?" one belligerent man at a corner table asked.

"Fraid so gentlemen," Horace confirmed as he reached for Jenny and gently placed her on the floor. "I need everyone to leave immediately. We have an urgent matter that needs tending to."

"Anything we can do to help?" a cowboy at the front of the crowd asked.

"Actually any help would be appreciated," Horace informed them. "Do you all recall the men that Jimmy escorted out of here last night?"

"The ones that were groping on Jenny and Millie?" another cowboy asked.

"Those are the ones," Horace confirmed. "Well, Jenny saw them lurking in the shadows outside the saloon from her balcony a little over half an hour ago and now Millie is missing."

The crowd of men sat in stunned silence for a full five seconds before they all started talking at once, but the resounding theme was "Count me in."

Jenny watched as the volunteers gathered around them and was touched that so many wanted to help find her friend.

"I'll be right back," Jenny told Horace as she made her way to the stair case.

"Where do you think you're going?" he asked.

"To change, so I can help find Millie," she replied while turning around and was surprised to see him right behind her.

"No Jenny," Horace said firmly. "You need to stay here."

"But Horace..."

"Jenny, you will just be in the way," Horace told her. "I can find Millie faster if I know you are safe here."

"Horace, I know you care for us girls, but..."

"It's different with you Jenny," he surprised her by saying. "I have to know you're safe. If you really want us to find Millie quickly you'll promise to stay here and wait."

Jenny couldn't make sense of everything he was saying, but she didn't have time to sort it all out right then, so she reluctantly agreed and watched as Horace and the men all filed out of the saloon to search for Millie.

'Oh God,' Jenny prayed as she slowly made her way up the stairs, 'please let her be alright!'

~*~*~*~

Horace wanted to explain everything to Jenny. He had wanted to tell her for a long time, but the timing was never right, and it certainly wasn't the right time now. Millie was one of his girls and it was his job to protect them, but he had no idea where to even start to look for her.

"All right men," he addressed the posse of assembled patrons, "I need four groups. We will head in four

~ 68 ~

different directions. If they have her they couldn't have gotten far. I am offering a one hundred dollar reward for the group that finds her first."

Shouts went up at that last part. One hundred dollars was a lot of money, but it would be worth every penny if it encouraged them to find Millie faster.

As they rode in all directions Horace cast one last glance toward the saloon. He had insisted Jimmy stay behind to guard the rest of the girls and especially Jenny. He needed to know she was safe.

Chapter 4

Jenny felt the hairs on the back of her neck stand on end and knew she wasn't alone. She turned quickly to find the sorry excuse for a man that she had danced with just the night before. He flashed a wicked looking blade at her silencing any thought of screaming. Anyone who heard her would never make it to her in time.

"What have you done with Millie?" she asked. Concern for her friend outweighed the concern for herself.

"Oh don't you worry," he chuckled, "Jonas is taking care of her."

"No," Jenny said as all the blood leached from her face and the room started to spin.

"That's right Darlin," the intruder crooned, "it's just you and me now. No more interruptions."

"Mr. you don't have to do this," Jenny tried to reason with him. "The Honk-Tonk isn't too far and there are plenty of women there that would be happy to oblige you and your cousin." She didn't bother to remind him they weren't welcome *there* anymore either.

"I don't want a *whore* tonight," Travis spat then smiled at her revealing a missing front tooth. "Rumor has it you're as pure as the driven snow and I aim to find out for myself if'n it's true."

"Please don't do this," she pleaded. If he didn't listen to reason there was only one way this was going to end. One of them would not be leaving this room alive and she prayed it would be him, but she would die before she would willingly allow his advances.

"Too late for that Darlin," he drawled taking a few steps closer, "but don't worry he assured her. I'm an expert at these things. The first virgin I took ended up marrying me or thinking she did anyway."

That last statement confused Jenny. How could any woman "think" she married a man?

"Now," he said pointing the knife at her chest, "first things first, I want to enjoy this. Your body has been haunting me for days and I want to watch you take every stitch of clothing off those curves of yours; starting with your dress."

Jenny's hand shook as she unbuttoned the silk gown and let it slide off of her shoulders and puddle at her feet. If she played her cards right his sick little game would work in her favor.

"That's right Darlin," crooned as he stepped forward and ran a finger along the edge of her chemise and the swell of her breasts. He swallowed hard and took a few steps back. "You're making this harder than I thought," he informed her as he wiped his mouth with the back of his sleeve. "Now, your garters and stockings."

Jenny had to fight to keep her face passive. This is what she'd been hoping for as she bent down and began to inch her petticoats up her right leg all the way to her thigh she stopped just short of relieving the jeweled dagger that she had strapped just above her garter. Most of the other girls carried derringers in their bosoms, but Jenny had never been comfortable with the weapon and when

~ 71 ~

Horace had given her the beautiful dagger he'd won in a poker match she'd practiced with it until she was deadly accurate. Only now did she wish she'd chosen a different weapon. If she had carried a derringer his knife wouldn't have been much of a match for it and he may have surrendered when she pulled it out, but as it was there was no way she could intimidate or wound the man in front of her and still make it out alive. No, the only way to stop this brute of a man would be to kill him.

With a prayer and reflexes that were lightning quick she pulled the dagger from its sheath and watched in horror and relief as the deadly weapon hit its mark.

Travis gasped in shock as the dagger hit dead center of his heart. He looked at her in wonder, took two steps toward her and collapsed in a heap at her feet. His blood pooled onto the dress she'd been wearing. Its color blending in with the shade of the dyed silk and she knew she'd never wear red again.

"Jimmy!" she screamed as she leapt over the dead body and threw open the door. She didn't even bother with a robe as she dashed down the stairs. "Jimmy!"

"Whoa there," Jimmy soothed as she ran smack into him and he caught her before she tumbled backwards. "Jenny what's wrong?"

"Jimmy, he's got her!" she wailed as she stepped out of his grasp and headed for the door. She didn't make it very far before Jimmy reached her and barred the way.

"Who's got who Jenny?"

"Jonas!" she cried, "Jonas has Millie!"

"How do you know?" Jimmy asked clearly thinking she was just distraught.

"Because Travis told me," Jenny told him trying to shove him out of her way.

"Jenny," Jimmy said gently grabbing her shoulders, "who is Travis?"

"He's the other man you threw out," she said in exasperation. "He snuck into my room and I had to kill him, but before I did he told me that his cousin, Jonas, has my Millie!"

The bouncer sat in stunned silence for what seemed like ages to Jenny.

"Jimmy, please get out of my way!" Jenny cried out in frustration. "I have to find Millie!"

"I'm sorry Jenny, but this is for your own good," Jimmy informed her just before he threw her over his shoulder and carried her upstairs. He didn't stop till he got to Goldie and Lylla's door. He didn't even bother to knock as he barged in their door. "Ladies, I need you to keep her here till either me or Horace comes for her."

Both of the women blinked at him in bewilderment for a moment, but Goldie was the first to recover.

"Sure thing Jimmy," Goldie said as Jimmy placed Jenny on her feet and bolted the door behind him.

The events of the day and all of Jenny's emotions seemed to close in on her at once and her legs gave out from under her as she collapsed into a sobbing heap.

Neither of the women asked any of the questions that were swirling around in their heads. Instead they just held her while she cried and when she seemed totally spent they helped her onto one of their beds.

~*~*~*~

Jenny couldn't seem to get away from him. Even with the dagger still protruding from his chest he refused to let her go. She could hear Millie screaming for her, but the man holding her had an iron grip.

"Millie!" she cried, "Millie I can't get free," she sobbed as her friend continued to scream.

"Shhhh," a gentle voice broke through the nightmare, "It's alright Love. You're safe."

A gentle hand bathed her forehead and arms with a damp cloth. The coolness of the cloth was pulling her from her dream, but she was afraid to leave Millie there.

"Millie," she whimpered.

"It's alright Jenny," she heard another feminine voice say. "Horace found her."

"Millie!" Jenny exclaimed as she bolted upright in bed and blinked at Goldie and Lylla. It didn't take long for the fog to clear. "Horace found her? Is she alright?"

The uneasy silence in the room didn't bode well and Jenny sprang from the bed before either woman knew she'd moved.

"Millie," she cried as she reached her room.

"Jenny?" Millie cried as she sat up and searched for her.

"Oh Millie," Jenny wailed as she took in her best friend's battered features. "I'm so sorry. I tried to warn you, but I was too late."

"It wasn't your fault Jenny," Millie assured her. "I was so worried about you! Jonas told me Travis was waiting for you in our room and I had no way to warn you."

"He was," Jenny shuddered at the memory and couldn't stop her eyes from wandering to the place where his lifeless body had been only hours before. The body and the dress were gone, but no amount of scrubbing would remove the blood that now stained the floor. "I had to kill him," she admitted.

She had never taken a life and she truly thought she would feel remorse, but instead she was just glad he couldn't hurt anyone else.

"Oh Jenny," Millie said in awe, "I'm so proud of you. I wish I could have killed Jonas, but he found my derringer and disarmed me before I had a chance to use it."

"Millie, did Horace find you before…before…" but Jenny couldn't finish the sentence as she saw great tears well up in Millie's eyes and she shook her head sadly.

"No," Millie whispered, "By the time they found me he was long gone."

"Oh Millie! Noooo!" Jenny wailed as she pulled her friend into her arms.

"I suppose Horace will send me away now," Millie sniffed after she and Jenny had cried in each other's arms for a good long while.

"If he does we'll go together," Jenny declared.

"No," Millie shook her head vehemently, "Jenny, all of Oak Springs thinks we're fallen women anyway, and the men that were with Horace when he found me know for sure that I'm fallen now."

"You are NOT a fallen woman Millicent!" Jenny scolded. "You did nothing to encourage that brute."

"Jenny, you know that's not the way the town will see it," Millie said sadly.

"I don't care how they see it!" Jenny exclaimed. "We'll find a new town."

"It won't work Jenny and you know it," Millie said stubbornly. "We've seen it before and we both know what's in store for me now."

"No!" Jenny cried, "I won't allow Horace to do this!"

"Won't allow Horace to do what?" the man in question asked as he came upon the heated scene.

"How could you even think about turning Millie out?!" Jenny screamed at him. "If she goes, I go!"

"Whoa!" Horace said holding his hands up. "No one is going anywhere."

"But Horace, you know it will be impossible to keep the men…"

"No it won't," Horace argued, "because neither of you are allowed to work the saloon…ever again."

"You can't turn Jenny out Horace! She hasn't…"

"I'm not turning anyone out Millie. You are both staying," Horace said firmly.

"But you said…"

"All I said was that neither of you are allowed to work the saloon anymore," Horace defended.

"But if we don't work the saloon how will we…"

Horace held up his hands to stop the barrage of questions. "I haven't exactly worked out the particulars," he said firmly. "All I know is that it is too dangerous for you two to work the saloon anymore. Until I do get it figured out I will pay you both a weekly salary for cleaning up the saloon after all the patrons have left, and even then you are only allowed in the saloon if Jimmy is there to watch over you."

"Horace don't you think that's a little too over protective?" Jenny asked while Millie sat in stunned silence.

"No!" he said surprising them both at his vehemence. "I want you safe and this is the only way I can see, to make that happen. Unless…"

"Unless what?" they both asked in unison.

"Nothing," Horace said, but his grin said he was up to something. "Jenny, can I talk to you in the hall for a moment."

"Sure Horace," Jenny said while sending Millie a puzzled look.

Once they had stepped into the hall Horace closed the door to their room so Millie couldn't overhear.

"Jenny, I need you to fetch the Dr. so he can examine Millie."

"Oh Horace!" Jenny exclaimed, "I can't do that to Millie. She has a terrible crush on him and I'm certain she won't want him to see her like this."

"Jenny, if she's hurt bad we need to know," Horace reasoned.

"I guess you're right," Jenny admitted begrudgingly. "I'll get dressed and head to his office."

"Take Jimmy with you," Horace warned.

"Horace, don't you think you're taking this a little too far?" she asked as he began to shake his head in denial. "Horace, I've walked these streets alone countless times before this with no trouble what so ever."

"Jenny, Jonas is still out there," Horace reasoned, "and you killed his cousin. He's not going to take too kindly to that. So until he's found I want you to be extra careful."

Jenny hadn't thought of it that way, and as much as she hated to admit it he was right.

"Alright," she agreed.

"Promise?"

"I promise," Jenny said begrudgingly and Horace chuckled.

"Good girl," he said as he headed for the stairs.

~*~*~*~

"Noooo!" Millie wailed as Jenny walked in with Dr. Michaels, "Did you have to ruin my best dream?"

"Millie, I had to get you some help," Jenny soothed as tenderly wiped her friend's tears away.

"But he thought I was a good woman," Millie sobbed.

"You are a good woman Millicent," Dr. Michaels announced as he knelt by the bed and took Millie's hand.

"You won't think so anymore," Millie wailed again.

"I'm sorry Dr. Michaels she isn't normally like this," Jenny apologized

"Jenny, I'm gonna have to ask you to step out of the room, so I can examine Millie," Dr. Michaels told her as he started rummaging through his medical bad.

"You'll call for me if you need me?" Jenny asked not sure she should leave Millie's side.

"I will," he promised.

"Are you going to be alright?" Jenny asked Millie.

"I would have been better if you'd left Blain out of this," Millie said sourly.

"You mean Dr. Michaels," Jenny corrected while glancing nervously at the doctor, but he looked as though he'd been handed the moon.

"No, that's alright," he assured her, "I'm glad she feels comfortable enough to call me by my first name."

Jenny shook her head in disgust and exited the room.

~*~*~*~

The next day found Jenny sitting beside Millie's bed as she read from a Bible that Dr. Michaels had given her. Jenny soaked up every word her friend read like a sponge. She was fascinated by the love God showed the world when he gave them His Son, and humbled that that Son would so willingly lay down His life for them.

Neither one knew how long they had been reading when they heard a knock on their door. Jenny was loathed to have their reading interrupted, but the knock sounded rather urgent.

"Can I help you?" she asked as she found a handsome dark haired, brown eyed, stocky youth of about sixteen years on the other side of the door.

"Yes ma'am," the boy said, "I'm looking for a Jenny McGreggor."

"I'm Jenny," she said smiling warmly at him.

"Hello Miss McGreggor, my name is Bobby Duggard and my dad sent me for you," he explained as his cheeks burned red. "He owns the saloon at the other side of town."

This was Harry's son? Jenny didn't even know the owner of the Honky Tonk had a son.

"What does he want me for?" Jenny asked in confusion.

"One of his girls is asking for you," he told her.

Jenny didn't know any of Harry's girls...save one.

"What's wrong with Darby?" Jenny asked as she got a horrible sinking feeling in the pit of her stomach.

"A couple of guys worked her over about a week back and she just keeps getting worse and worse," tears filled the boys eyes as he whispered, "I don't think she's gonna make it. In truth ma'am, my dad doesn't know I'm here, but I love Darby and I can't deny her this last request. Please say you'll come."

Jenny's heart felt like it was being ripped from her chest. "Of course I'll come."

"Oh, thank you Miss McGreggor," the boy said releasing the breath he'd been holding. "I hope you don't mind, but I'll need you to carry this with you," he said holding out a large, colorful, quilted bag.

Jenny didn't know what to make of the bag, but when he added "please" she found she couldn't resist and accepted the awkward gift from him.

Chapter 5

Jenny had never been inside the Honky Tonk before, and she was eternally grateful that Horace had insisted on escorting her there and back. At first he had tried to talk her out it altogether, but when he saw that she was determined he gave up and went with her instead.

The boy led them up the stairs of the filthy establishment and into a dark room.

"Darby," he whispered softly, "she's here."

"Oh Bobby!" a frail voice cried, "I knew you would do it. Please open the drapes and let the light in. I want to see her."

Jenny watched as the boy crossed the room and drew open the drapes, allowing the afternoon sunset to flood the tidy little room and illuminated the small figure in the bed.

"Jenny!" the once beautiful girl cried.

Jenny had to fight back tears as she went to Darby's side. Gone was the healthy, rosy glow of just months before. Even her honey colored hair seemed to have taken on the grey pallor of death.

"I wasn't sure you'd come," the girl said in awe.

"Of course I came," Jenny said reaching for her hand.

"I wasn't sure you would even remember me," Darby said shyly. "I am less than a nobody."

"That's not how I see you and that's not how God sees you either," Jenny assured her.

Then all of the sudden it made sense! The story was personal! God didn't just love the world, He loved Jenny and Jesus didn't just die for the world he died for Jenny and… Jenny looked down at the girl beside her and couldn't stop the flow of tears…he died for Darby.

"Darby, I need to tell you about someone and I need for you to listen," Jenny pleaded.

"I need to tell you about someone too," Darby told her while sending a look to Bobby. "I need everyone to leave us please."

"Alright Sweetheart," the boy said and ushered everyone out of the room leaving Jenny alone with Darby and Bobby.

"You go first," Darby urged.

Jenny sent up a prayer for guidance as she began to tell the age old story of how their marvelous Creator loved them so much that he couldn't bear to be separated from them. She told Darby about the Gift of salvation through believing in God's one and only Son.

"But I don't understand," Darby said as her fevered brow knit in confusion. "Why would He want me? No one's ever wanted me."

"Well, He does," Jenny assured her, "He wants you so badly that He died for your sins."

"Oh Jenny!" Darby cried as great tears filled her eyes, "I want to belong to him, but I don't know how."

"The Bible says if we confess with our mouths and believe in our hearts we'll be saved."

Jenny had no idea that she was going to be leading someone to Christ as she found the way herself, but she knew she would never be the same again as she, Darby, and Bobby accepted the Lord as their Savior.

"Now," Darby smiled weakly at Jenny, "there is someone I want you to meet. Would you please bring him to me Sweetheart?" she addressed Bobby and Jenny watched as he moved a floor board by the bed and brought out a tiny bundle.

Jenny sat in awe as he carefully laid it on Darby's chest and sucked in a sharp breath as she peeled back the blanket to reveal one of the tiniest babies she had ever seen.

"Isn't he beautiful?" Darby asked in wonder.

"Oh Darby," she breathed as she reached out and ran one finger along his smooth cheek, "he perfect."

"We were planning on running away together," Darby said and Jenny knew she was speaking of her and Bobby, "but it doesn't appear that I'll be running anywhere."

"Don't say that Darby," Jenny begged, "I'll go get Dr. Michaels. He'll fix you up…" but Darby just shook her head sadly.

"No Jenny," she denied, "I've been hemorrhaging for almost a week now. There has been so much blood. I'm just thankful that I had given birth a few days before…before…or well, this precious little one wouldn't be here."

"I tried to get my dad to let me get the doctor, but he said whores were a dime a dozen and he wouldn't spend a nickel on them," Bobby sobbed as he dropped to his knees beside Darby. "I'm so sorry Sweetheart. I wish we had run away sooner. We could have been married by now."

"Don't cry Bobby," Darby said as she placed a hand on his cheek. "At least we know we'll be together again someday."

Tears flowed down Jenny cheeks as she watched the boy place a gentle kiss in Darby's palm.

"Do you have the bag?" Darby asked Jenny.

"Yes," she replied holding it up for the girl to see.

"I need to ask something of you," Darby said weakly, "I need you to take our son and find him a couple that will love him."

"A couple that will love him as their own," Bobby said as he bent down to place a gentle kiss on the dark downy hair covering his son's head.

"I...but...you..." Jenny couldn't seem to find the words.

"Please Jenny," Darby begged as tears filled her eyes, "He is the most precious thing we have. We need someone we can trust to find him a home."

"We don't want him to end up in an orphanage," Bobby added.

Jenny knew she couldn't deny them this, "Alright," she agreed. "I'll find him a home."

The young parents' relief was obvious. "Thank you," the sighed in unison. Then she watched as Bobby and Darby both picked him up and bid their precious son goodbye.

"Place him in the bag Bobby," Darby said through her tears as she handed her son back to his father.

"Why does he need to go into the bag?" Jenny asked.

"Because Harry can never find out," Darby told her.

"He would just use him against me," Bobby explained. "He would tell everyone the baby was his to force me to stay and work for him."

Jenny had never had a very high opinion of the Honky Tonk's owner, but right now he was right up there with a snake's belly.

"You must go now," Bobby said after he'd placed the newborn in the bag and handed him to her. "I don't want you to be here when my dad gets back."

Jenny didn't even try to hold back the tears as she bid Darby goodbye for the last time on earth and stepped out into the hall where Horace was waiting.

~*~*~*~

Once they made it back outside and into the sunshine Jenny took a deep breath of cleansing air. She longed to take the baby out of his bag so he could breathe the fresh air too, but she didn't dare.

"All this time," Horace was the first to break the silence as they walked back to the better part of town, "I had no idea what kind of life I was sending those girls to."

"How could you have known?" Jenny asked, but secretly she was thinking the same thing.

"I should have done something different," Horace said then let out a weary sigh, "but then again I've made so many mistakes in my lifetime. When a man gets to be my age he starts to wonder what he's contributed to the world."

Jenny didn't know how to respond so she just kept silent. Horace was at least twenty years her senior, but he wasn't nearly as old as he was making himself sound.

"I want to make a difference," he announced, "I'm tired of this lifestyle. I've been thinking about selling out for a long time now, but I haven't a clue what to do, or where to go next."

"If you sell out what will happen to us girls?" Jenny asked in bewilderment. Horace had always seemed hard as nails, but something had changed in the last few days.

"Don't you worry Sweetheart," Horace smiled at her, "I would never abandon you."

Jenny felt a little uncomfortable. Horace had been making strange comments on and off since she started working for him, but in the last week they seemed to becoming more frequently. She cared for Horace, but not in a romantic way. There was only one man she'd ever loved and she was pretty sure she would love him till the day she died.

She had just opened her mouth to tell him when a pitiful mewing sound came from the bag she was trying so hard not to jostle around.

"What in the world?" Horace said as his eyes flew to the quilted bag. "Jenny what do you have in the bag?" he demanded.

"I can't show you here," Jenny told him while her eyes pleaded with him to understand.

"Then don't show me. Tell me."

She knew she wasn't going to be able to keep the baby a secret from him now anyway, and she let out a sigh as she said, "It's a newborn baby Horace."

Jenny had to fight to keep from laughing at his horrified expression. After all what did he think made that sort of sound?

"Jenny what…how…" Horace stuttered.

"It's Darby and Bobby's son," Jenny explained and told him everything that had transpired after he left the room.

"So you told them about a God I didn't even know you knew, and they just gave you their baby?" he asked incredulously.

"No," Jenny said patiently as she gently swayed the bag back and forth to quiet the baby within. "They called me there to give me their son and to ask me to find him a home, but before they did I told them about God."

"Hum…" he said as he raised one brow in concentration. "Where are you going to find a couple to adopt him? You and I aren't exactly welcome in polite company, and I'm sure you wouldn't want to give him to anyone we associate with."

"Maybe no one *you* associate with," Jenny said with an unlady like snort, "but I already have someone in mind and as soon as she lays eyes on this beautiful baby boy I think my search will be over before it began."

"Really?" Horace asked in surprise. "Who?"

"I need to stop by the seamstress shop on the way home," Jenny said with a smile.

~*~*~*~

The bell jingled overhead as Jenny walked into the front door of the Nip and Tuck.

Jenny was glad that Horace agreed to let her visit alone, but he made her promise not to leave until Jimmy showed up to walk her back.

"Elizabeth," she called to her friend before she had a chance to emerge from the backroom where all the sewing was done.

"Jenny!" Elizabeth cried in surprise, "I'm so glad you came by! I've been so worried. How are you doing? How is Millie? Oh I was just sick when I heard about what happened."

"I'm fine," Jenny giggled as the questions poured from her friend.

"How is Millie?"

"Well...she's going to take a few days to heal," Jenny answered honestly while all mirth vanished, "but I just came from the Honky Tonk, and after seeing the poor girl those lowlifes got to first I'd say that Millie is lucky."

"Oh no," Elizabeth breathed as her hand went to her mouth. "Is she going to be okay?"

Tears filled Jenny's eyes as she shook her head sadly. "No, I'm afraid she's not."

"Oh Jenny, I'm so sorry," Elizabeth exclaimed as she pulled her friend into her embrace bumping the colorful bag by accident, and jumped back when the infant wailed his protest. "What on earth?"

Jenny walked to the backroom without a word and after placing the bag onto Elizabeth's worktable, pulled the beautiful, baby boy out and handed him to Elizabeth.

"Hello there Sweetie," Elizabeth cooed to the baby as she rocked him. After the enchantment wore off a little she looked expectantly at her friend.

Jenny told her everything. Starting with how she met Darby months ago, right down to the moment she walked into the shop.

"How wonderful God is to have worked this all out," Elizabeth said in wonder. "Your paths crossed months ago so you could be there for her in the end. Not only did you lead her to Christ, but you found Him yourself."

"I know," Jenny agreed.

"Do you have anyone in mind for this handsome little man?" Elizabeth asked the million dollar question.

"Well I was hoping you and Eric…"

"Oh Jenny," Elizabeth exclaimed sending her friend an apologetic look, "I would love to take him, but you see…I'm pregnant. We haven't announced it yet."

"Elizabeth that is wonderful!" Jenny exclaimed as she hugged her friend. She was disappointed that the baby still needed a home, but she knew Elizabeth and Eric had been trying for a baby for a while now.

"I'm sorry I can't take him," Elizabeth told her as she snuggled the baby closer.

"Me too," Jenny agreed. "You wouldn't happen to know anyone that would take him and love him as their own; maybe someone that can't have kids of their own."

"No, I don't know any..." Elizabeth's eyes lit up as she bounced up and down a little. "Yes I do! I do know someone!"

"That's great!" Jenny giggled at her friend's enthusiasm. "Who?"

"My husband's sister had a baby girl a little over a year ago," Elizabeth explained. "During birth she had some complications and now she can't have anymore. They are wonderful parents and they are looking for a little boy to adopt."

"That's perfect!" Jenny exclaimed. "Where can I find them?"

"They live in Riverview," Elizabeth informed her and watched as Jenny blanched. "Jenny, are you alright?"

"Yes," Jenny said while willing her pulse to slow down.

"Are you sure?" Elizabeth asked obviously unconvinced

"Yes I'm fine," Jenny assured her. She could do this. If it meant getting that precious baby to a loving family she could do anything. "They sound perfect. How soon do you think they could take him?"

"I'm sure they could take him right away," Elizabeth enthused, "I'll contact LeAnn and arrange all the details."

"Oh thank you Elizabeth!" Jenny exclaimed. "I really appreciate this."

"Think nothing of it." Elizabeth laughed and whispered to the infant in her arms, "In truth I'm doing it for purely selfish reasons. This way I get a new nephew in the bargain and this Auntie loves nieces and nephews."

Jenny laughed at her friend's antics. She could imagine Elizabeth was a terrific aunt, and she would be an even better mother.

It wasn't until later that evening that reality sunk in, and she wasn't sure whether she was excited or terrified.

"I'm going home," she said in awe. What if she ran into Trevor? Would he even remember her? Would he be married? It would be absolute torture to learn that the only man haunting your dreams was out of your grasp forever. At least here, safely tucked away in Oak Springs, Jenny could pretend that he would one day be hers, but what if all her dreams became nightmares?

Chapter 6

Jenny stepped off the train in her new, navy blue traveling suit. Elizabeth had insisted on it and three other dresses. Jenny had tried to pay her for them, but Elizabeth had insisted that it was her contribution toward placing her new nephew in his new home.

It felt good to blend in with the other women and felt even better that no one knew what she was here.

Millie was the only one besides Elizabeth and Eric that knew where she'd gone. She didn't dare tell Horace for fear he'd insist on accompanying her, and this was one trip she was determined to make alone.

Jenny took a good look around and was immediately transported back in time. Nothing had changed. Riverview was almost exactly as she had remembered it from so long ago.

The same old shops and businesses like Thompson's Mercantile, the town bank, the Riverview Bed and Breakfast, and the jail all sat on one side of the red clay street and on the other side sat what used to be Dr. McKinney's office. Next were Pop's Barber Shop, and Mr. Allen's Smithy and Livery. A red school house with black trim was the town's only new addition that she could see.

At the north end of town sat the white clapboard church that she and her parents had attended when she was a girl, and to the south the Red River meandered along oblivious to the lives depending on it.

"Home," she breathed and had to fight back tears. When she'd left Riverview almost six years ago she didn't think she would ever see it again, but now the memories came flooding back.

"Miss McGreggor?" a male familiar male voice interrupted and Jenny whirled around with the infant in her arms. It was Trevor's older brother and he had the most enchanting little moppet in his arms.

"Luke?" Jenny couldn't believe how much he'd changed, but he was still just as handsome as ever and she would have recognized him anywhere.

"Yes," Luke smiled at her as he stuck out his hand, "I'm Luke Rollins and this," he said as he pulled the most beautiful woman Jenny had ever seen forward, "is my wife LeAnn. Elizabeth told us when to be expecting you."

He didn't remember her? Of course he didn't remember her. She was just a girl the last time he saw her, and now here he was married; and to Elizabeth's sister-in-law of all people.

'What a small world,' she thought to herself.

"You *are* Jenny McGreggor?" he asked as he eyed her and the infant uncertainly.

"Yes," she rushed to assure him, "Yes, I'm Jenny McGreggor, and I do believe you are here for this little man," she said as she held the baby out to LeAnn.

"Oh Luke," LeAnn breathed as she accepted the infant and tears filled her eyes. "Isn't he beautiful?"

"He most certainly is Sweetheart," Luke agreed as he wrapped his free arm around his wife's shoulders and peered down at his new son.

Jenny had to blink back tears. How she wished Darby could have seen the picture the newly enlarged family made. She had no doubt that God had led her to this couple. They were a perfect match for the precious little angel she'd been entrusted with.

"What's his name?" LeAnn surprised Jenny by asking.

"He doesn't have a name yet," Jenny admitted.

"Adam," LeAnn sighed and smiled up at Luke.

"Adam," Luke agreed. "Adam Quincy Rollins, just like we agreed on before we had Aisley."

"I love it," Jenny told them honestly. "His parents would have loved it too."

"Thank you so much for bringing him to us," LeAnn beamed at her.

"You're more than welcome," Jenny assured her. "Would you mind if I came by and said goodbye to Adam before I left?"

"What do you mean came by?" LeAnn asked as she furrowed her brow. "You're coming home with us."

"Oh no," Jenny began, but was quickly cut off.

"There's no way I'm going to allow you to stay in town when you've gone so far out of your way for us," LeAnn informed her.

"But I don't want to impose..." she tried to reason with the couple, but was cut off again.

"Best not to argue with her," Luke laughed and winked at her, "take it from me."

"Oh I don't know," Jenny said doubtfully. "Are you sure?"

"I won't have it any other way," LeAnn announced as she grabbed Jenny's hand and started pulling her toward a waiting wagon.

"But my luggage," Jenny said.

"Don't worry, Luke will get it. Won't you Sweetheart?" LeAnn assured her sending her husband a charming smile.

"Of course," Luke chuckled as he sat Aisley in the back of the wagon, "what kind of a gentleman do you take me for?" he teased.

"Oh I can't wait till this evening," LeAnn gushed, "the whole family is getting together to meet you and this little fella."

"The whole family?" Jenny felt like she was going to faint and LeAnn was so excited that she didn't notice when Jenny started to sway. She shouldn't have come. She wasn't ready for this. She needed to go home. Now!

"Whoa," a pair of strong arms wrapped around her just before her knees gave out and the world went black.

~*~*~*~

"Jenny?" Trevor said in awe as he cradled the woman of his dreams in his arms.

'Scratch that,' he thought to himself, 'his dreams simply didn't do her justice.'

"You know her?" LeAnn asked in confusion.

"I love her," Trevor corrected.

"Oh! I should have recognized the name," Luke exclaimed as he neared the wagon with Jenny's one suitcase and a stuffed, large, quilted bag. "She's your Jenny."

Both Trevor and LeAnn looked at him as though he'd grown two heads.

"She is isn't she?" Luke asked Trevor.

"I can't believe you remembered," Trevor told his brother.

"Of course I remembered!" Luke snorted. "How could I forget your biggest crush? You moped for weeks after she left."

"Jenny isn't just a crush Luke," Trevor snapped, "and I've mourned her every day she's been gone."

"Hey," Luke said gently, "I didn't mean anything by it Little Brother."

"How come no one ever told me about any of this?" LeAnn demanded.

"Later Sweetie," Luke promised turning his attention back towards his brother as Jenny started to stir.

Trevor held his breath as Jenny's eyes fluttered open and she smiled at him.

"Hurry up and kiss me Trevor before Millie wakes me up again," she shocked him by saying, but it didn't take long for him to snap out of it as his lips claimed hers.

At first she stiffened as his lips touched hers, but it didn't take long for her to start responding in turn and Trevor felt it down to his toes. She moaned as he deepened the kiss and he knew he was lost.

~*~*~*~

Jenny had been shocked when she actually felt his lips on hers. This was no dream! Trevor was holding her and he was kissing her and nothing had ever felt so good.

She tried to make sense of it all, but her muddled brain refused to work with him kissing her like that and she couldn't stop the moan that escaped.

"Ah Hum," Luke cleared his throat rather loudly.

Jenny missed his touch the moment he pulled away and sat her on her feet. Her cheeks flamed red as she noticed the crowd of onlookers that had gathered around to watch.

"Why don't you come on over Trevor?" Luke suggested with a grin. "I think you and Miss McGreggor have some catching up to do."

"I think I will," Trevor replied as Jenny chanced a shy look his way.

'My, but he's a handsome man,' Jenny thought to herself.

The hair peeking out from under his Stetson had gone from dark blond to brown, but he still had the same kind, mischievous, doe brown eyes she remembered. She would have known him anywhere by his eyes alone.

Gone was the boy of yesteryear and in his place was one of the biggest men she'd ever seen. The clean white shirt he wore stretched taut over his back, chest and biceps. While the jeans he wore hugged thick powerful legs.

Jenny was quite certain there wasn't a more handsome man in all of Texas, or in all the world for that matter.

What did he think of her?

~*~*~*~

'Sweet heavens, she's a sight to behold!' Trevor couldn't stop thinking to himself.

Her eyes were still the same striking topaz he remembered and her hair still reminded him of a new copper penny. Her skin was smooth as cream, and Trevor was pleased to see she still had the dusting a freckles across the bridge of her nose. A beautifully tailored traveling suit hugged some very feminine curves she'd acquired since he'd last saw her. While a matching hat sat at a jaunty angle on top of the copper curls pilled high on her head.

"You're even more beautiful than I remember," the words were out of his mouth before he could stop them, not that he had tried that hard, "and that memory was pretty hard to beat."

To his delight she turned a pretty shade of pink.

"Alright you two," Luke intruded again, "let's finish this up in the privacy of our own home."

Trevor glanced around and noticed they were drawing quite a bit of attention. He imagined the news would travel like wild fire. Everyone in town had been trying to set him up with a sister, daughter, cousin or grandmother it seemed, and now he'd just gone and kissed a woman smack dab in the middle of town for all to see! He wasn't sure he'd live this one down.

He glanced at Jenny again and grinned. It was totally worth it!

~*~*~*~

The ride to Luke and LeAnn's place didn't take long, and Trevor dismounted quickly so he could help Jenny down. He felt like he was still in a dream as he set her on her feet and she smiled shyly up at him.

"Unca Trebor!" a little voice demanded and Trevor turned around just as Aisley launched herself out of the wagon. He caught her and spun her around while she giggled with glee. "Wee!"

Jenny watched the interaction between Trevor and his niece and couldn't help but feel a pang of remorse. If her parents had lived she would have been part of this family by now. She would be an aunt, and maybe even possibly a mother. She blushed at the idea and chanced a look Trevor's way. Her blush deepened when she locked eyes with his and could tell that his thoughts mirrored her own.

LeAnn led the way into the house still cradling little Adam.

No sooner had he closed the door when Trevor turned to Jenny and blurted out, "Jenny, will you marry me?"

"Trevor I..."

"Oh please say you will," he pleaded. "Jenny, I've loved you for all of my life and I'm scared to death that if I turn around you'll vanish. Say you'll marry me and we'll go right now to the preacher."

"Whoa there Romeo," Luke intervened. "Look, I know you two have feelings for each other, but a lot can happen in five years. Maybe you should take the time to get reacquainted before making a decision that big."

"It doesn't matter how long it's been, or what's happened," Trevor argued. "I loved her five years ago and I love her today. She's the only woman for me."

Jenny was stunned. He loved her. She wanted more than anything to marry him, but she knew Luke was right. There was much that Trevor didn't know about her and she wasn't sure she was ready to share just yet.

"Trevor, I love you too," she wanted him to know his feelings were reciprocated, "but Luke is right. It *has* been a long time, and we should get to know one another again."

"Okay," Trevor agreed reluctantly, "but just promise me you won't vanish again."

"I promise," Jenny said as she reached up and placed her palm on his smooth cheek. Trevor captured her palm and placed a gentle kiss in it sending tingles from the point of contact all the way down to her toes, just before weaving his fingers with hers.

"Well, now that that's settled," LeAnn giggled, "would you like to come meet your new nephew Trevor?"

"I would love to," Trevor replied, but refused to let go of Jenny's hand as he inspected the newest member of the Rollins family. "He's beautiful LeAnn."

"Isn't he though?" LeAnn gushed as she nuzzled her new baby's soft cheek.

"We named him Adam," Luke chimed in as he reached for his new son for the first time, and his wife reluctantly relinquished her hold.

"Baby," a tiny voice said and everyone looked down to find Aisley pulling on her father's pants leg as she held her little arms out and waited expectantly.

"Bubba," Luke corrected as he knelt down for Aisley to see. "This is your new baby brother Sweetie."

Everyone laughed as she plopped down on the floor and patted her lap, "Baby."

Jenny felt like her heart would explode as Luke sat on the floor next to his daughter and placed her little brother in her tiny arms.

"Watch his head," LeAnn warned as she too knelt by her daughter to support Adam's head.

"Me baby," Aisley said proudly as she beamed at them all.

"Yes Sweetie," LeAnn agreed as she bent down to place a soft kiss on Aisley's brow. "He's your baby."

Chapter 7

Jenny should have felt out of place, but instead she just felt like she'd come home as she was ushered into the Rollins' family homestead. Of course it helped that she was by Trevor's side.

Inside it was a wonderful mix of rustic and feminine. The home itself was made of cedar, and inside the log walls were polished to a shine. It was all one large open room down stairs. That included the dining room, kitchen, and a sitting space that sported a mammoth sized fireplace. A plush, brown leather divan sat directly in front of the fireplace with matching love seats flanking both sides. A large chest overflowing with toys sat in the front corner of the room beside the cold fireplace. Colorful rag rugs graced the pine plank floors and sheer white lacy curtains fluttered at the windows.

"Boy, am I glad you guys finally made it," Seth informed them as soon as they entered the house. "Your mother has been driving me crazy all day. She is beside herself with excitement."

"Where is she?" LeAnn asked. "I can't wait for her to see him. Have my parent's arrived yet?"

"She's in the kitchen," Seth chuckled as he watched LeAnn take off in the direction of the kitchen, "and no your parents haven't made it yet."

"I don't think she even heard that last part," Luke laughed as he watched his wife's retreating figure.

"Me either," Seth agreed then his brows rose as he turned toward his youngest son and the woman he was holding hands with.

"Dad, you remember Jenny McGreggor," Trevor said praying it was true, but the puzzled look his father sent his way wasn't very promising.

"Dad," Luke intervened, "this is *the* Jenny McGreggor."

"The Jenny McGreggor?" then as it dawned on him he exclaimed, "*The* Jenny McGreggor! You're all grown up!"

"Yes Sir." Jenny said bashfully.

"It's so good to see you," Seth answered truthfully, but inside he had a thousand questions rolling around in his head.

"You too," Jenny replied as she smiled up at Trevor.

"Seth!" Ruby exclaimed as she entered the room carrying her new grandson. "Seth! Have you seen our beautiful new grandbaby?"

"Not really Sweetheart," Seth chuckled as his wife brought the bundle forward and held him out to his grandfather. "LeAnn whisked him away to you the moment they stepped through the door."

"Sorry about that Dad," LeAnn said sheepishly.

"I wouldn't have expected any less," Seth winked at her as he accepted his grandson. "He's a sport isn't he?"

"Isn't he though?" Ruby enthused, but a glance Trevor's way sobered her right up. "Jenny?"

"Hello Mrs. Rollins," Jenny couldn't begin to explain how pleased she was that Trevor's mom remembered her.

"Jenny!" Ruby exclaimed as she drew Jenny into her embrace. "It's so good to see you!"

"It's good to see you too Mrs. Rollins," Jenny answered sincerely.

"How…"

"She brought Adam to us," Luke explained before his mother could voice the question.

"Then I'm doubly glad you're here," Ruby exclaimed as she gave her a quick, impulsive hug. "Isn't he beautiful?" she asked as though Jenny didn't know.

"Yes Ma'am he is," Jenny agreed with a laugh.

"Nana!" Aisley squealed as she launched herself out of Luke's arms and into her grandmother's.

"Why hello there precious," Ruby laughed as she caught her oldest grandbaby. "Have you been a good girl?"

"Me baby," Aisley said proudly as she pointed to her brother.

"My baby," her mother corrected, "Can you say "my baby" Aisley?" but Aisley just stuck her thumb in her rosebud mouth and grinned.

"I see you have a new baby," Ruby said. "Can you say Bubba?"

"Bubba," Aisley repeated solemnly.

"That's right Dearest," Ruby encouraged as she pointed to the baby, "Bubba."

"Bubba," Aisley agreed as her little hand reached out to gently touch her brother's downy, soft head and then squirmed to get down.

"Would you ladies mind helping me in the kitchen," Ruby asked as she placed Aisley on her feet and the little girl toddled toward the corner of the living room and the chest full of toys.

"I would love to," Jenny replied. She couldn't remember the last time she'd been in a kitchen. She had always enjoyed cooking.

"Me too," LeAnn chimed in.

"Wonderful!" Ruby said as she led the way to the kitchen.

~*~*~*~

Trevor watched Jenny until she disappeared through the kitchen doorway.

"Okay you two," Seth said as soon as the women were in the other room, "would someone like to enlighten me?"

"We haven't figured it all out ourselves," Luke answered honestly, "but I can tell you what I know. You already know about Elizabeth contacting us about Adam, and you know that a woman was supposed to meet us at the train station today with him. But none of us knew who the woman was, and to be honest we didn't think it would matter."

"Oh it matters," Trevor chuckled. "It matters a lot."

"How did you come to be at the train station?" Luke asked his brother.

"I came to meet my new nephew and as I was approaching I saw LeAnn chattering away to a swaying woman," Trevor explained, "so I ran up and caught her just as she fainted and got the surprise of my life when I saw that the woman in my arms was none other than *my* Jenny."

"He kissed her right there on the street in front of everyone!" Luke guffawed.

"You did what?" Seth asked his son incredulously.

"Well...she told me to," Trevor defended sending his brother a sour look.

"Then when we got to my house..."

"Really Luke!" Trevor cried in exasperation.

"...he proposed!" Luke finished and laughed till he cried.

Trevor turned beet red as his father shook his head in disbelief.

"You proposed to her?" Seth asked in astonishment.

"Who proposed to who?" Katie asked as she walked in with Brooke on her hip.

"Oh great!" Trevor groaned as Luke started laughing again.

"It's a long story Kitten," Seth told Katie, using her pet name.

"Oh don't worry," Trevor snorted in disgust, "Luke won't have any problem telling you all about it."

With that he stormed past a bewildered Lance on his way out.

"What on earth is wrong with Trevor?" Lance asked as he joined the group with Blake in tow. "I don't think I've ever seen him angry before."

Seth and Katie turned and looked pointedly at a shamefaced Luke.

"I know," Luke said sheepishly.

"No son," Seth told his oldest son sternly, "you don't know. That boy has loved that girl since he was just eight years old. You never took it serious and to tell you the truth I didn't either, but I think it's time to face the facts. You don't hold onto a memory like that if it's not love."

"I recon your right," Luke agreed. "When we were younger I couldn't fathom that he was actually in love. I had never been in love and I just didn't take him seriously, but I have no such excuses now. If someone were to make light of the way I feel about LeAnn…well I'd be angry, and it's plain to see his feelings for Jenny are just as strong as mine."

"Jenny's here?" Katie asked in disbelief.

"Appears so," Seth confirmed.

"Oh Luke!" Katie groaned, "You teased him about Jenny?"

"I know," Luke ducked his head as he headed for the door, "I'm going to make it right."

"You'd better," Katie warned.

"Boy, you're getting bossy in your old age," Luke threw over his shoulder with a laugh as he headed out the door after his brother.

"Who's Jenny?" Lance asked.

~*~*~*~

Trevor was still seething when his brother walked up and leaned on the coral next to him.

"Luke so help me for your safety and my sanity I suggest you go away," Trevor warned. "I feel like throttling something and if you're not real careful it may just be you."

"I would deserve it," Luke said softly.

"You sure would," Trevor agreed sourly.

"Look Trevor, I'm really sorry," Luke began," and not just for today, but I'm sorry for not being there for you five years ago. I was old enough to go after her for you, but I just never dreamed..."

"That little brother was in love?" Trevor finished for him and snorted in disgust. "I wasn't a baby then and I'm certainly not a baby now Luke."

"I know that," Luke told him. "I should have backed you up. I should have done so much more back then and...I should have said so much less today. I truly am sorry Trevor."

Trevor took a deep breath and let it out slowly, and with it went all his pent up anger.

"I know it don't count for much Little Brother," Luke continued, his voice thick with emotion, "but I've got your back now."

"Thanks Luke," Trevor smiled at him. "It counts a lot."

"What do you say we go back inside so I can get to know my future sister-in-law better," Luke suggested.

"I can't believe she's in there," Trevor said in amazement as he looked toward the house. "I've dreamed of her so many times that I keep thinking any moment now I'll wake up."

"I can fix that," Luke assured him.

"Ow!" Trevor yelped as Luke gave his arm a good pinch.

"Yep you're awake," Luke laughed as he tore off toward the house with a laughing Trevor hard on his heels.

"Oh are you gonna get it," Travis shouted as he started to close the gap.

"Just trying to help," Luke laughed as he and Trevor burst through his parents' front door.

"Boys, what on earth?" Ruby exclaimed as she sat a platter of pork chops on the table.

"He started it Momma," Trevor informed his mother.

"I didn't do anything, but try to be a good, supportive brother," Luke defended.

"Well now you can both be good, supportive sons and get the babies cleaned up while we finish setting the table," Ruby threw over her shoulder as she went back to the kitchen for more food.

"Now look what you did," Trevor teased.

~*~*~*~

Jenny couldn't remember when she'd had such a good time. She was thrilled that Katie remembered her. She had always liked Trevor's sister, and her twins were the sweetest little things.

She was seated next to Trevor at the table and they held hands through almost the entire meal.

Conversation flowed easily and Jenny loved how everyone laughed and cut up. LeAnn's parents fit right in and Jenny wondered if her parents had lived would they have been around the table too? But then again the whole reason everyone was gathered together in the first place was to welcome little Adam into the family, and if her parents had been there she would never have met Darby and who knew where the precious infant would have ended up.

Jenny missed her parents, but she would be eternally grateful that she had been able to be there for Darby, Bobby and Adam.

Her father was always telling her that God worked in mysterious ways and for once in her life she could see what he meant. She hadn't been then, but she was thankful now for the Christian home she'd been raised in. Jenny only wished that she had paid more attention back then. Maybe she wouldn't have been so devastated when they'd died if she'd had the hope she now had of actually seeing them again.

After the meal was over and the dishes were done Trevor asked her to take a walk.

Jenny's heart pounded as they stepped off the front porch steps hand in hand and started walking toward the river. This was the man she loved. The man she wanted to spend the rest of her life with. If it hadn't been for her past she would have married him earlier that day, but Trevor had a right to know what kind of woman he was marrying before he made that kind of a commitment.

Once they reached the river Trevor led her to a fallen log that had been carved into a bench. Jenny knew the time had come. Before she allowed this to go any further she needed to tell him.

"Trevor, I feel like I'm in a dream," Jenny broke the companionable silence.

"Me too Jenny," Trevor said as he turned to face her and tucked a stray copper curl behind her ear. "A dream I've dreamed over, and over, and over again."

"I'm sorry about earlier," Jenny said and Trevor knew by the pink creeping up her neck that she was referring to her request in town.

"I'm not," Trevor chuckled.

"I'm not exactly sorry about the outcome," Jenny admitted with a giggle.

"I can't believe you still have this," Trevor said as he touched the ring on her right hand.

"I've only taken it off once," Jenny admitted, "to have it resized."

"Oh Jenny," Trevor breathed as he pulled her into his arms and just held her. "I can't tell you how much I've missed you. You're the best friend I've ever had and the only girl I've ever loved."

"Trevor Rollins, I'll love you till the day I die," Jenny sighed.

"Marry me Jenny," Trevor said as he leaned her back, so he could look into her eyes. "You promised to long ago."

"I did promise," Jenny smiled at him sadly, "but there are some things you need to know about my past, and you may decide you don't want to marry me."

"There is nothing in your past that can keep me from wanting you for my wife Jenny Lynn McGreggor. All I'm asking for is your future." Trevor assured her and groaned just before his lips came crashing down on hers.

The feel of Trevor's lips sent her senses reeling and she whimpered as he pulled her into his lap and trailed kisses down her chin and neck. They weren't kids anymore, and her body came alive in ways she didn't even know it could. Jenny shivered as he found her earlobe and then her lips again.

"Marry me Jenny," he growled against her neck. "I can't live without you. Marry me."

"Yes," Jenny moaned as he started kissing her neck again. "Yes, I'll marry you."

"When?" Trevor stopped his sensual assault long enough to ask.

"Soon!" Jenny laughed as she scrambled to get off his lap, then gave him a mock stern look, "Until then I think we should use more restraint."

"I'm just making up for lost time," Trevor teased as he rose from the bench and slowly started to stalk towards her.

Jenny laughed as she made a break for the house, and let out a little shriek when Trevor's strong arms wrapped around her waist.

"Don't you ever run from me again Jenny Lynn McGreggor," Trevor chuckled as he turned her around and gave her a kiss that curled her toes.

"That will be hard not to do if that's going to be my punishment," Jenny teased.

"If you like that then just wait and see what happens when you don't run," Trevor promised as he led her back to the house.

~*~*~*~

Ruby insisted Jenny stay with them and Jenny gratefully accepted. She wasn't looking forward to intruding on the Luke's family during this special time.

It wasn't until she was in bed that she realized what she'd done. She'd agreed to marry Trevor and he didn't even know he was getting a saloon girl in the bargain. There was no way she would start out their new life that way. If she was going to be Trevor's wife then they needed to be totally honest from the start.

The next day was Sunday. A day she had been looking forward to since the day she knew she was coming home. Now it was a day she was dreading. She would have to tell him after services and pray he still wanted to marry her.

Chapter 8

Trevor couldn't wait to get to church this morning. He'd been so excited about Jenny yesterday that he'd almost forgotten that Bro. Andrews had asked him to fill in today since he and his wife were going to be out of town until Tuesday. He couldn't wait to present her to the congregation as his fiancé.

If it were up to him he would have Jenny on Bro. Andrews' doorstep to perform the ceremony first thing Wednesday morning. His mom had convinced him to give Jenny at least a month's time to prepare for the wedding and since he wanted Jenny to have a real wedding he reluctantly agreed.

In the mean time it was agreed that Jenny should stay with his parents until the wedding.

He also planned to talk to her about taking her back to wherever it was she'd come from to get her things, and to take care of any business that needed to be handled. It occurred to him that not only did he not know where she lived, but he pretty much didn't know anything else either. That was something he intended to start rectifying today. He wanted to know everything about her.

Duke, Trevor's huge black and white painted stallion was already saddled for him before he made it to the livery. The smithy's son, Jarrod, was a stocky lad, only ten years of age, but he was a hard worker and followed Trevor around trying to mimic him.

Jarrod remind Trevor of himself at that age, and he enjoyed being around the youth.

"Thanks Jarrod," Trevor said as he ruffled the boy's hair and mounted his horse. "Will I see you at the services this morning?"

"I don't think so Mr. Rollins," Jarrod admitted as he ducked his head.

Mr. Allen was a good man, but he was a lost man. Trevor had been trying to witness to him off and on in the two year's time he'd been apprenticing under him, but to no avail.

"Well, if you change your mind I'd love to see you there," Trevor told him sincerely. "I'm preaching today."

"You're preaching today?" Jarrod asked in amazement.

"Sure am," Trevor said sending the boy a wink. "Sure would love to see you there."

"I'll try Mr. Rollins," Jarrod promised.

"I'll keep an eye out for you," Trevor assured him with a smile just before he set off toward the church.

~*~*~*~

Jenny was a nervous wreck. She'd already gotten ready for church once, but during breakfast she accidently spilt her coffee effectively ruining one of her new dresses. Then to make matters worse she'd burst into tears and made a fool out of herself.

She was in the middle of giving herself a good sit down when she heard a soft nock on the door.

"Jenny," Ruby called softly. "May I come in?"

"Just a second," Jenny called as she quickly dashed the tears from her cheek. "Come in."

"Honey are you…" Ruby's heart broke for this woman that was about to become her daughter in law. She didn't know what was in her past, but it was plain to see that it was haunting her.

Jenny didn't resist as Ruby pulled her into her arms and held her. Nor could she stem the torrent of tears.

"Oh Mrs. Rollins I love him so much," Jenny sobbed.

"Well that's a good thing Honey," Ruby soothed.

"You don't understand," Jenny said as she slightly pulled away to look into Ruby's eyes. "I'm…I'm not good enough for him."

"Honey that isn't the way Trevor sees it," she assured her.

"That's because he doesn't know," Jenny wailed. "I was going to tell him when he kissed me senseless and then I couldn't remember my own name much less what I needed to say."

"The boy takes after his father," Ruby chuckled as she led Jenny to the edge of her bed and pulled her down beside her. "Now, what is it that he doesn't know that you think will matter so much?"

Jenny had to tell someone and if anyone knew how Trevor would react it would be this woman.

"Mrs. Rollins for the past five years I've worked as a dance hall girl," Jenny admitted refusing to look at the appalled expression that was sure to gracing Trevor's mother's face. "When my parents died I had nowhere else to go. My Aunt and Uncle wanted to send me to an orphanage, so I ran away. I know you won't see it this way, but even then God's hand was on me. I ran into a man named Horace and went to work for him. He doesn't allow any...any...well you know. It could have been much worse. I only had to dance for my living, other girls in town aren't so lucky. I know what you must think of me and..."

"Oh you poor girl," Ruby sobbed as she gathered her into her arms. "I'm so sorry. We should have gone after you. Trevor tried to, but Seth caught up to him in Oak Springs and brought him back. For two days Trevor didn't eat or sleep. I was worried and was getting ready to approach Seth about it Katie disappeared and I'm ashamed to say I forgot all about Trevor's distress and you."

"Trevor went after me?" Jenny asked incredulously.

"Yes," Ruby smiled sadly, "he did."

"He was in Oak Springs?" Jenny couldn't believe he'd been that close and she didn't even know it.

"Were you in Oak Springs?" Ruby asked certain she already knew the answer.

"That's where I've been for the past six years," Jenny admitted. "I never wanted this life, but I didn't know where else to go, or what else to do."

"You were just a girl," Ruby said as she tenderly wiped away Jenny's tears. "You shouldn't have had to find your own way. I'm so sorry."

"It wasn't your fault," Jenny assured her. "Do you think Trevor..."

"I don't think there's anything you could say to my son that would change his mind about marrying you Jenny Lynn McGreggor," Ruby laughed.

"Really?" Jenny asked still a little uncertain.

"Trust me honey," Ruby said as she patted Jenny's hand and stood. "Now I think we better get you ready for church."

Jenny looked down helplessly at the dark spot staining her new green dress. "I only have two more dresses with me besides my traveling suit," Jenny admitted.

"Let me see them," Ruby encouraged.

Ruby watched as Jenny pulled out a pink calico day dress and then a beautiful yellow and white striped silk creation that only could have come from Elizabeth.

"This one," Ruby said holding up the yellow silk gown.

"You don't think it's too much?" Jenny asked uncertainly.

"Not at all," Ruby said already laying it out for her. "I'll help you get into it."

~*~*~*~

Trevor knew the moment his parents wagon came into view, and he wasted no time as he weaved through the crowd gathered on the church's lawn. He was waiting at his parents normal parking spot before they'd even reached it.

"Good morning," he greeted as he reached for Jenny's trim waist and sat her on her feet.

"Good morning," Jenny beamed at him and Trevor couldn't seem to draw a full breath.

"Is it just me or have you gotten prettier since last night?" he teased. But in truth she did look especially beautiful with her hair all piled on top of her head. A few daisies scattered throughout her copper curls were the perfect complement to her bell style, sunny yellow, silk dress. Its bodice fit her to perfection, the fitted sleeves went to her elbows where Brussels lace belled out almost to her wrists and the modest boat neckline was outlined in matching lace that drew his eyes to the smooth column of her neck. A neck he'd kissed just the day before. His mouth went dry at the memory.

"I think it's time for church to start son," Seth chuckled as he nudged Trevor.

"Oh!" Trevor didn't know how long he'd been staring at his fiancé, but he figured there were a lot worser things he could be doing with his time and grinned unrepentantly as he offered Jenny his arm.

~*~*~*~

My, oh my, but Trevor looked good in his black suit and matching black Stetson! Jenny found it hard to breathe as he sat her on her feet.

'This man wants to marry me,' she thought to herself in amazement. She had to be the luckiest woman in the world! She wanted to throw her arms around him and kiss him right there, but the church lawn was no place for that, so instead she just stood back and drank in the sight of him.

She felt like the buttons on her dress might pop off as she took Trevor's arm and he led her toward the church building for services. She couldn't help but notice that they were drawing a lot of attention and she wondered if anyone remembered her.

Jenny was glad she'd talked to his mom earlier. It had put her at ease and now she was once again looking forward to the service. She was still a little nervous about talking to Trevor, but nothing like she'd been before. She believed with all her heart that this was the man God had for her, and she would just trust Him to make everything right, or that *had* been the plan.

The singing was wonderful and Jenny enjoyed hearing Trevor's deep baritone voice beside her. She was anxiously waiting for the sermon when the song leader announced that the pastor was out of town and the associate pastor would be filling in today. Excitement went through the congregation and Jenny found herself excited with them.

'He must be a good preacher,' Jenny thought to herself based on the reaction of those around her. Then she watched in horror as Trevor stood up and took the place behind the pulpit. 'Noooo!' Jenny's heart screamed as he asked everyone to open their Bibles.

It was bad enough that she was going to have to tell him about her past, but it was beyond cruel to learn that there was no way they could have a future together because of it.

Jenny couldn't marry a preacher. There was no way anyone would accept him as a man of God if he married her and Jenny would never ask him to choose her over God.

She had no idea what the sermon was about as she had to fight the tears of anger, hurt and frustration through the entire service. By the time it came to a close she was exhausted with the effort.

"Before I dismiss everyone I have an announcement to make," Trevor told the congregation just before the closing prayer.

'Oh Father I can't do this!' her heart cried as she stood up and flew out the church door.

"Jenny!" she heard Trevor call after her.

She knew Trevor wouldn't stop until he found her. That's why she bought a horse from the Livery and left Riverview before he'd even made it out of the church yard.

Tears streamed down Jenny's face as once again she left behind the only man she'd ever loved.

~*~*~*~

Trevor was so torn. He knew he had a job to finish, but he had to go after Jenny.

"I've got it Little Brother," Luke said as he stood up and made his way to the front of the church, "go after her."

Trevor didn't need to be told twice as he sent his brother a grateful look, excused himself and tore out of the church in search of the woman he loved.

Once out in the church yard he took a quick survey of the wagons and tried not to panic when he walked all the way around the church and still didn't find her. The congregation had been dismissed and the families heading home by the time he mounted Duke and spurred him toward town. If he had to tear every inch of Riverview apart he'd find her.

"She's gone!" Trevor announced to his family as he burst through his parent's door.

"What do you mean she's gone?" Seth asked trying to recover from his shock.

"I mean she bought a horse from Allen and she's gone," Trevor replied as he ran his hands through his hair in frustration.

"Why would she just leave?" LeAnn said in bewilderment.

"I don't know," Trevor snapped.

"I do," Ruby shocked them all by saying.

"Why Momma?" Trevor asked in a strangled voice.

"She was going to talk to you later this afternoon, but I think she panicked when she realized you were a preacher," Ruby began.

"What was she going to tell me that would cause her to panic when she found out I was a preacher?" Trevor asked in confusion.

Ruby took a deep breath, "I really wish this had come from her, but I guess it will have to do coming from me."

~ 122 ~

Tears filled the giant man's eyes as his mother told him about Jenny's past, and the entire family was speechless.

"I've gotta find her," Trevor said as he headed for the door. "I want a wife and I'll have no other. I don't care if she'd been a prostitute; nevertheless a dancehall girl!"

"Wait for me!" Luke yelled springing to his feet and racing for his horse after giving LeAnn a quick kiss.

"Me too!" Lance chimed in as he kissed Katie and followed Luke out the door.

"You don't have to go," Trevor told his brothers as he mounted Duke.

"I'm doing what I should have done five years ago Little Brother," Luke informed him as he climbed up into Bucky's saddle

"And I'm doing what I would have done if I'd known you five years ago," Lance chimed in as Storm pranced under his weight. "Besides you need a tracker and that's something I happen to be really good at."

"Thanks," Trevor said sincerely, "I need to stop by the house and change my clothes."

"Me too," both of his brothers said in unison.

"Alright, after you guys change out of your suits meet me at the livery," Trevor instructed them.

"Sounds like a plan," Luke agreed.

"We'll find her Trevor," Lance promised as they all went their separate ways.

~*~*~*~

It was late that evening when Jenny pulled up to the only Hotel Pecos Texas had to offer. She knew she must look a sight. She'd cried most of the way and her eyes felt like sand paper. She was beyond exhausted and prayed that this particular establishment didn't have bedbugs.

She was relieved to see that everything appeared fairly clean as she made her way to the desk.

"Excuse me," she said getting the attention of a tall, slender woman.

"Hello," the woman greeted with a smile. "Can I help you?"

"Yes Ma'am I need a room for the night," Jenny said grateful for the warm welcome.

"Sure thing," the kind woman said as she reached for a key. "Just one night?"

"Yes Ma'am," Jenny confirmed, "I'm taking the train to Oak Springs tomorrow morning."

"Wonderful," the woman bubbled handing Jenny her room key, "if there's anything I can get for you don't hesitate to ask."

"Actually, I was hoping I could get someone to knock on my door around seven." Jenny told her. "I'm normally up by then, but I'm so tired I'm not sure I won't sleep through."

"Don't you worry," the woman assured her, "I'll do it personally. You just go on and get some rest."

"Thank you. I need to take my horse to the Livery and then I intend to do just that," Jenny informed her with a tired smile.

"No need for that," the woman said, "is that little gray mare yours?"

Jenny nodded her head, "Yes Ma'am"

"I'll have my husband take her on over to the livery for you and you can get her in the morning."

"Oh, bless you," Jenny sighed.

She didn't quite remember making it to her room, and she was asleep before her head had fully hit the pillow, but the sleep was wrestles at best. In her dreams brown eyes accused her and all that she'd lost haunted her.

Jenny almost felt worse when the knock came for her to get up than when she'd arrived last night. Fresh tears were near the surface, but she stubbornly fought them back. There'd be time for that when she got home.

She cleaned her face, and tried to bring some order to her unruly curls before heading down stairs to check out. After eating what she could of her breakfast at the local diner she set off in search of the livery. It wasn't hard to locate and in no time at all she had collected her mare and boarded the train. She knew it was foolish to keep the horse, but she couldn't bring herself to leave anything else behind.

~*~*~*~

Trevor had hated to stop for the night, but darkness had been descending on them quickly and everyone had needed to rest.

He'd been hoping to make it to Pecos before nightfall, but he'd wasted too much precious time looking for Jenny in Riverview. They were only about half way there when they headed out again, just as the sky was beginning to promise daylight.

"How does Elizabeth know Jenny?" Trevor broke the silence.

"I'm not sure," Luke admitted, "Elizabeth didn't say much. All we knew was that a friend of hers was given the task of finding a home for our Adam and asked if we wanted him. Of course that was a no brainer."

"Do you know how Jenny ended up with him?" Lance asked.

"No," Luke answered, "we were going to find out more about everything when she brought him to us, but well I'm afraid she was rather distracted when she got there." Luke chuckled and grinned at his brother.

"Are you saying I'm the distraction?" Trevor teased.

"No, of course not!" Luke laughed.

"You can't believe how shocked I was when I caught her," Trevor told them.

"I can imagine," Lance assured him. "You might have felt a little like I did the first time I saw Katie by the river in an Indian dress. I think my heart skipped three full beats!"

"Or you might have felt a little like me when LeAnn was shoved in my lap and looked at me with those beautiful violet eyes for the first time," Luke sighed. "I thought an angel had fallen from heaven!"

"Or maybe I felt like a man in the middle of the dessert, dying from thirst, so sure that the oasis in front of me was just another mirage," Trevor said softly.

Chapter 9

The train left Pecos at exactly eight in the morning, and once again Jenny found herself fighting tears.

"What is wrong with me!" she berated herself as she stubbornly dashed the wetness away.

This was for the best. She knew he would come after her this time and she knew she would have to convince him that she didn't want him; something she wasn't sure she could pull off.

She went over and over the scenario at least a hundred times in her mind before the train pulled into the Oak Springs station. By the time she stepped onto the station platform she felt in control of herself and confident that she could do what needed to be done.

After her new horse was safely ensconced in a stall at the Livery she made her way back to Horace's Place.

"Where have you been?" Horace demanded the moment she entered the saloon. "I've been worried sick!"

"I'm sorry Horace, but I had to take Adam to his new family," Jenny explained.

"Who is Adam?" Horace asked.

"Darby and Bobby's baby," Jenny informed him, "The new family named him Adam."

"You shouldn't have gone alone," Horace scolded. "I would have gone with you."

"I didn't want anyone to go with me," Jenny retorted. "It was something I had to do on my own."

"Why?" Horace demanded.

"Horace, I appreciate what you do for me," Jenny snapped, "but you don't own me!"

Horace took a deep breath and let it out slowly, "I know I don't own you Jenny, but I do care about you and I just want to be sure you're safe. If it hadn't been for the fact that the authorities captured Jonas I would have went after you."

"Horace, I care for you too," Jenny told him, "but...well...as a friend."

Horace laughed out loud, "Sweetheart, I love you way more than a friend," he admitted, "but not in a romantic way."

"What other way is there?" Jenny asked in confusion.

"Take a walk with me?" he asked offering her his arm. "The things I need to tell you shouldn't be said in a saloon."

Jenny hesitated for a moment, but took his arm and allowed him to lead her out of the saloon and away from the town's businesses. She wasn't afraid of Horace. She knew that he would never hurt her or allow anyone else to for that matter.

"Jenny, I knew the first time I saw you who you were," Horace admitted as he stopped and turned to her with tears in his eyes. "I should have done so many things differently," he paused as he took a deep breath, "starting with the day your mother told me she was pregnant with you."

"Told you she was..." Jenny's eyes went round with shock. "Why would she tell you..."

"Because…because I'm your father Jenny," Horace admitted.

"No," Jenny whispered in denial.

"It's true Jenny," Horace assured her as she jerked her hand away from his arm. "I loved your mother, but when I found out she was pregnant I had to make a choice. There was no way I could keep my reputation spotless and my girls in line if they knew that you were mine."

"So you chose to keep your saloon over my mom and me?" Jenny accused.

"I know it was wrong," Horace assured her, "I should have told you long ago."

"Why would you do that?" Jenny asked as she began to shake with furry. "If no one knew I was your daughter you could make a sleazy dance hall girl out of me!"

"Jenny I…"

"NO!" Jenny screamed, "Do you realize what you've done?! You've ruined my life! You have ruined my chances at a life! At *the* life! The life that I want, the man that I love!"

"Jenny, I'm so sorry," Horace's eyes pleaded with her to forgive him.

"It's not enough," Jenny said just before she ran off.

~*~*~*~

Jenny didn't know how she made it to Elizabeth's, nor did she know how Millie came to be there, but there she was pouring her life's story out to her best friends.

~ 129 ~

"Wow! Jenny," Elizabeth exclaimed when Jenny had finished her tale. "You're in love with Trevor Rollins?"

"Horace, is you father?" Millie asked in amazement.

"It appears so on both accounts," Jenny told them. "Of course I can't marry Trevor and there's no way I can forgive Horace!"

"Why can't you marry Trevor?" Millie asked.

"You have to forgive Horace Jenny," Elizabeth said gently.

"No, I don't," Jenny denied, "and you know why I can't," Jenny said addressing both questions at once.

"Jenny, the Bible teaches us that we have to forgive if we want to be forgiven," Elizabeth told her.

"How?" Jenny asked. "How do I forgive something so terrible?"

"Jenny…" Elizabeth paused trying to find the right words to say, "You said that you already had a dad."

"That's right," Jenny confirmed, "John McGreggor has been my dad since I was seven years old."

"Did you love him?" Elizabeth asked.

"I still do," Jenny said softly.

"Was your mother happy with him?" Elizabeth asked.

"I think I know where you're going with this," Jenny sighed. "Yes, my mother and father were very much in love till the day they died, but what about the rest of my life? He knew I was his daughter and instead of doing the right thing he made me a dancehall girl!"

"He also fed, clothed and protected you fiercely," Millie added softly. "Maybe at the time he did the best he knew how to do."

"It's true," Elizabeth added, "You can't expect a lost man to act like a saved man."

"But he's ruined my chances at a real life," Jenny argued.

"You can still have a real life," Millie informed her. "If Trevor really loves you he'll marry you anyway."

"What decent man wants to marry a saloon girl?" Jenny asked sarcastically.

"Well…." Millie and Elizabeth exchanged smiles. "The doctor for one."

"What?" Jenny asked in amazement. "Does Dr. Michaels want to marry you?"

"No," Millie giggled, "Dr. Michaels did marry me!"

"They were married yesterday," Elizabeth explained to a shocked Jenny.

"You're married?" she asked incredulously. "How?"

"Well, the day after you left I started to get sick," Millie blushed, "and when Blain examined me he found out I was pregnant…"

"No," Jenny gasped.

"At first I was devastated," Millie admitted, "I didn't know what I was going to do. There was no way I was going to be able to be a "respectable" dancehall girl anymore"

"Oh Millie," Jenny breathed, "I'm so sorry."

"I'm not," Millie shocked her by saying. "The next day Blain asked me to marry him and took me to stay with Elizabeth and Eric until we said our vows yesterday. He said a baby is a blessing from God in any form and that we would love it and raise it together. He is so wonderful," Millie said as she sighed dreamily.

"Millie, that is wonderful!" Jenny exclaimed as she embraced her friend. "I'm so happy for you!"

"So see," Millie laughed, "if I can marry Blain you can marry your Trevor."

But Jenny just shook her head sadly, "No, it's not the same," she told her friend. "There's a big difference between a saloon girl marrying a doctor and marrying a preacher."

"Jenny," Elizabeth said reaching for her hand, "if Trevor's not the one for you, then God has someone out there who is. There is no reason for you to have to stay a saloon girl."

"But I don't know what else to do," Jenny admitted helplessly.

"Why don't you come work for me?" Elizabeth offered.

"I wouldn't have a clue how to help you," Jenny told her.

"I can teach you," Elizabeth assured her friend, "and until you learn you can help with clean up, which just happens to be my least favorite part of sewing," she said with a wink.

"You would do that?" Jenny asked in awe. "What about the town. You might lose customers if you hire me."

"Nonsense," Elizabeth exclaimed with an unladylike snort. "Where else are they gonna go, and I don't care if I do lose a few. If they are that petty I'm not sure I want their business anyway."

"What about Eric?" Jenny asked.

"What about Eric?" Elizabeth asked. "He isn't going to care. I do this because I love it. Not because I have to. He doesn't care how I run it."

"Are you sure?" Jenny asked one more time.

"Positive," Elizabeth assured her. "Go get your things and we'll get you set up in the upstairs apartment."

"Oh Elizabeth!" Jenny exclaimed, "I can't tell you how much this means to me."

"I'll close up shop while you go get your things," Elizabeth told her.

"I won't be long," Jenny promised as she practically danced out of the shop.

"Thank you Elizabeth," Millie said after Jenny had left. "She'll make you a good seamstress."

"She won't get the chance to learn," Elizabeth giggled.

"What do you mean?" Millie asked in shock.

"If I know Trevor Rollins the way I think I do, he won't be far behind," Elizabeth assured her. "I shouldn't be surprised if our little Jenny isn't a married woman herself before the days out."

"You really think so?" Millie asked in amazement.

The bell jingled as someone walked in and both women headed to the front.

"Well, hello there Trevor Rollins," Elizabeth sang out as she spotted the goliath man standing in her shop with Luke and Lance bringing up the rear, "I bet I know who you're looking for," she said with a wink.

"Where is she?" Trevor wasted no time in asking.

Jenny knew she wasn't alone when the hair on the back of her neck stood on end, and she whirled around at the sound of the door shutting.

"Trevor," she squeaked as she moved her hand to her heart to slow its rapid beat, "how..."

"After I tore Riverview apart, I tracked you to Pecos," he told her as he slowly made his way toward her and stopped just short, "then I had to ride like a crazy man to get here before nightfall, and I'm not leaving this town without you as my wife."

"I want you to leave Trevor," Jenny tried to keep the quiver out of her voice. She had to convince him she didn't want him.

"Tell me you don't love me," Trevor demanded.

Jenny felt tears burn her eyes, but she refused to let him see them.

"I don't love you," she said firmly.

Trevor's eyes narrowed and he slowly stalked toward her until he had her backed against a wall.

"Your lips may say you don't love me, but your eyes say differently," he said bending down till his lips were a hair's breadth from hers. "Then again maybe your lips just don't know any better."

"Trevor please," she pleaded before his lips came crushing down on hers. At first she gave a feeble attempt to resist him, but the feel of his lips on hers had her senses reeling and she found herself kissing him back just as fiercely.

Jenny moaned as he pinned her against the wall and trailed kisses down her jaw and throat.

"I love you Trevor Rollins," the words were out before she could stop them and he lifted his head to gaze down at her.

"I know you do," Trevor whispered as he ran one finger down her smooth cheek, "and I have loved you for years. I can't live without you. Don't you see? Your past doesn't matter to me. I only ask that you give me your future."

"I'm not good enough for you Trevor," Jenny argued as the tears she been try to hold back finally slipped from her eyes, and ran down her cheeks, "no one will ever take you seriously as a preacher if you take a saloon girl for a wife. Everyone will think you've married a whore."

"Jenny Lynn McGreggor, you are not a whore," Trevor said fiercely cupping her face in his hands. "You had no choice over your situation and who better to be at my side then one who can sympathize with the lost. Together we can serve the Lord Jenny."

"But what if you regret it later?" she whispered.

"Jenny Lynn, the only thing I'll ever regret is that I didn't find you sooner," he assured her and Jenny let out a little shriek as Trevor gathered her in his arms and carried her out of the saloon without a backwards glance.

"Where are we going?" Jenny giggled.

"To find the preacher," Trevor informed her as he walked with determined strides toward the church with Jenny still in his arms.

When they got to the church Luke, Lance, Eric, Elizabeth and Millie were all there waiting.

~ 135 ~

"How did you know?" Trevor asked finally setting Jenny on her feet, only to grab her hand.

"How long have I been your brother?" Luke teased.

"All my life I guess," Trevor laughed.

"I knew," Luke assured him with a grin, and then turned and gestured to everyone else, "and the rest followed."

"I got him," Blain said as he walked up with Oak Springs' pastor in tow.

"I hear we're gonna have ourselves another impromptu wedding," he chuckled. "Those seem to be my specialty of late."

"I would be much obliged," Trevor said as he stepped forward and extended his free hand toward the pastor.

"I'd be glad to," the preacher laughed as he pumped Trevor's hand.

"Before we start the ceremony I have something for Jenny," Elizabeth announced. "I need you to come with me."

Trevor looked at her uncertainly and Elizabeth laughed, "I promise not to let her out of my sight!"

"And I promise not to run away ever again," Jenny assured him as she reached up on tip toe and pulled his head down to place a quick kiss on his lips, then disappeared into the church with Elizabeth and Millie.

"I see you swept her off her feet," Luke teased.

"Wasn't going to take no for an answer this time. Huh?" Lance chimed in.

"Yes," Trevor laughed turning to Luke, "and no," he continued to laugh turning to Lance. "That woman is going to be my wife."

The first thing Jenny saw when she entered the tiny room of the church near the entrance was a beautiful wedding dress.

"Elizabeth, how did you…"

"A woman ordered it about three months ago, but last week she informed me that the wedding had been called off," Elizabeth explained. "I believe the Lord intended it for you all along."

"I don't deserve it," Jenny said with tears in her eyes as she reached out and touched the snow white satin.

"I disagree," Elizabeth argued, "and I believe God does too."

Jenny felt like she was in a fairytale as her two best friends in the whole world slipped the wedding gown over her head. If she could have chosen any dress in the world to wear on her wedding day this would have been it.

The satin, ball gown dress had a short train, and short, semi puffed sleeves that hinted at falling off the shoulders. Exquisite embroidery accented the neckline, waist and hem. Tiny pearl button marched all the way down her back and down her train; while a wide satin sash wrapped around her tiny waist and made a large bow in the back. There was no lace, and no other beads, save the buttons. It was simply elegant.

"I don't know what to say," Jenny admitted as she stared at her reflection. "How can I ever repay you?"

"You can't," Elizabeth told her flatly, "Luke already did."

"Luke bought my dress?" Jenny asked in shock.

"Sure did," Elizabeth laughed at the memory, "I wanted to give it to you, but he insisted that he wanted to buy it as a wedding gift for his new sister-in-law."

Jenny didn't know when she had been so touched by a gesture.

"I'm sorry I don't have a veil for you," Elizabeth admitted. "I hadn't had a chance to start on it yet."

"I'm kind of glad you don't," Jenny surprised her by saying. "I want to wear my hair down."

"Oh Jenny," Millie exclaimed, "I've never seen you wear your hair down before and it's so beautiful. I know Trevor will be pleased."

The women had just finished fixing Jenny's hair when a knock sounded on the door.

"Who is it?" Millie called through the door.

"It's Lance," Jenny's other soon to be brother-in-law called back.

"You can come in," Millie giggled as she let the handsome half-breed in.

"I hope you don't mind, but I went over to the Lonestar Hotel and...well..," he said bashfully as he pulled a bouquet of yellow daffodils and white hyacinth from his back, "I got these for you."

As soon as the blossoms were offered, their fragrance filled the room.

"Oh Lance!" Jenny exclaimed as she stepped forward and received the beautiful, fragrant gift, "It's a perfect wedding bouquet. Thank you."

"You're welcome," Lance smiled at her. "You look beautiful. Trevor's a lucky man."

"Thank you again," Jenny sighed, "but between you and me, I'm the lucky one."

~*~*~*~

"I'm one lucky man," Trevor said out loud as Jenny stepped into the church. There was no music save that in his heart as he watched his bride glide gracefully down the aisle.

He'd dreamed of this moment thousands, maybe even millions of times since the day he'd met her over twelve years ago, and none of them could hold a candle to the real thing.

Her hair was a riot of copper curls cascading down her back past her bottom. The sides were pulled back and tiny blossoms from the hyacinth were scattered through her hair. He didn't know how Elizabeth produced such a beautiful dress in such a short time frame, but it was perfect for his gorgeous bride and he felt like his heart would explode with all the love he had inside for her.

"Words cannot describe how beautiful you are Jenny. I can't believe God brought you back to me. Next to His Son you are the most precious gift he has ever given me," he told her sincerely. "I promise to love you till the day I die and even through eternity."

"Trevor, you are the most wonderful, honorable, handsome man I have ever known, and I can't believe you want to marry me," Jenny told him as tears filled her eyes, "but I promise to spend the rest of my life here on earth and through eternity loving you. I'll bear your children, work by your side and I'll never leave you again."

"Well, that sounded like wedding vows to me," the preacher chuckled, "do you have the rings?"

"I have a ring," Trevor said as he pulled out the beautiful topaz ring his mother had given him and slid it on Jenny's finger.

"I love you Trevor Lee Rollins," Jenny beamed at him.

"And I love you Jenny Lynn Rollins," Trevor smiled back as he gathered her in his arms and kissed her before the preacher gave him permission.

"I guess you may kiss the bride," the preacher laughed as whoops, shouts and laughter went up around the newlyweds. "May I present, Mr. and Mrs. Trevor Lee Rollins.

~*~*~*~

Everyone, save the preacher, ended up at the Lonestar Hotel for dinner that evening.

The meal Mary, Elizabeth's mother, cooked was wonderful as usual, but if you'd asked Trevor what he ate he wouldn't have been able to tell you. He was just ready to be alone with his new bride and it seemed like it was taking forever.

He wanted to shout for joy when everyone finished and they all made their way to the lobby where Luke procured a room for both he and Lance for one night and another for Trevor and Jenny for two nights.

"You didn't have to do that," Trevor told his brother. "I could have paid for our room."

"I know, but this is my wedding gift to you." Then Luke said winking at his brother as he whispered conspiratorially, "Trust me you won't be in any hurry to go anywhere for a couple days."

"I don't recon so," Trevor chuckled as he looked at the woman he was ready to make his wife in every sense of the word.

~*~*~*~

Jenny had never been inside the Lonestar hotel before and was in awe of just how beautiful it was. She couldn't believe Elizabeth's parents owned it.

"It's beautiful," Jenny smiled at her friend.

"It sure is," Millie agreed.

"I was raised here," Elizabeth told them as she tried to see the hotel through her friends' eyes, "so I guess I kind of take it for granted, but it is beautiful."

The floor was made of a deep mahogany wood that had been polished to a mirror shine. The gigantic ornate rug both she, Millie and Elizabeth stood on was woven in varying shades of blue and decorated the center of the room. A huge chandelier hung from the center of the ceiling above the rug and the powder blue, velvet upholstered, ball and claw furniture that was arranged on it. The men stood near a mammoth sized matching mahogany colored desk served as the check in counter, and had a beautiful blue, tiffany lamp on it.

Jenny's breath caught as she locked eyes with Trevor across the room. That was her husband, and the look he was sending her sent her heart racing and her pulse pounding.

"Good night," Elizabeth giggled as Eric whisked her away.

"Don't be afraid Jenny," Millie whispered. "It really is wonderful."

"I'm not afraid," Jenny assured her with a smile, "and I'm really glad you're not with all you've been through."

"With Blain there was nothing to fear," Millie sighed as her new husband started her way. "I'm so in love with that man it's scary," she giggled.

"Oh Millie, I love you so much. I'm beyond happy that you have Blain," Jenny told her as she pulled her best friend in for one last hug before Blain could whisk her away.

It would have been hard to step into a happily ever after if her best friend had, had to remain in a nightmare. Only the Lord could have brought it all about so perfectly.

"Are you ready?" Trevor asked startling her out of her thoughts.

"I am if you are," Jenny assured him.

"Oh Honey," Trevor chuckled, "I'm more than ready."

Jenny giggled as he picked her up and carried her up the stairs to their room. He didn't set her down until he'd kicked the door shut behind them.

Jenny looked around the beautiful room and noted that the mahogany wood and blue theme, from down stairs, carried throughout this room too.

A set of long lace curtains fluttered in the breeze as if beckoning them over to the open French doors, and out onto the spacious balcony. A huge, canopied feather bed sat in the center of the room, upon another large ornate rug. The foot of the bed pointed towards the balcony, and was flanked on either side by nightstands, graced with lacy doilies and the same blue tiffany lamps as the one on the clerk's desk. A wash stand with an intricately painted bowl and pitcher sat just to the right of the French doors. To the left sat a matching table with a large vase full of daffodils and hyacinth that filled the entire room with their wonderful scent and made Jenny think of the sweet gift Lance had given her earlier.

A royal blue dressing screen graced the left back corner of the room, and in the center of the right wall two beautifully carved rocking chairs faced a large stone fireplace.

"It's beautiful," Jenny smiled up at him.

"You're beautiful," Trevor whispered as he cupped one side of her face and gently stroked her cheek with his thumb.

"Mmmm," Jenny sighed as she leaned into his touch.

"I love you Jenny Lynn Rollins," Trevor said softly as he gently ran the fingers of his free hand through her hair. "I think I've loved you from the first day I saw you walk into the school. I can't believe you're finally mine."

"I love you too Trevor," Jenny replied as she reached up on tiptoe and kissed her husband. It was just a slow sensual assault at first as she gently caressed his lips with her own.

"Oh, my sweet Jenny," Trevor groaned as he cupped her face in his hands and took the lead. Jenny willingly followed as the assault became all out war; each demanding more from the other in response.

Jenny's senses were reeling and she wasn't sure her legs could hold her up much longer by the time he finally let her up for air. A moan escaped and her head fell back as his lips found her neck and ears.

"Trevor," Jenny whimpered and squirmed against him when she didn't think she could take any more of his sensual onslaught.

"Did I hurt you?" Trevor asked in concern as he searched her face.

"No," Jenny assured him and giggled shyly, "Would you like to help me out of my wedding dress?"

"Sweetheart, I thought you'd never ask," he growled low as he gently turned her around and his fingers found their way to the buttons of her gown.

Chapter 10

Trevor was sure he was dreaming when he opened his eyes and saw Jenny beside him, but the feel of her warm body was all the proof he needed that this Jenny was all too real.

"Mmmm," Jenny said as Trevor snuggled up to her.

"Good morning Sweetheart," he chuckled.

"I'm dreaming aren't I?" Jenny giggled as she tried to blink the sleepy fog away.

"I know a way to convince you that you're not," Trevor assured her as he started to nibble on her ear.

"Shouldn't we get dressed for breakfast so we can see Luke and Lance off," she asked breathlessly as every nerve in her body stood on end and her pulse started to race.

"Nope," Trevor surprised her by saying, "I already told them not to wait around on our account."

"Trevor you didn't!" Jenny laughed while she struggled to get away.

"Oh no, you're not going anywhere Mrs. Rollins," Trevor promised as he pinned her on the bed and began his assault anew.

"Trevor," Jenny moaned, "won't they think were rude."

"Luke said he wouldn't expect anything less," Trevor assured her as he lifted his head and sent her a wicked smile and then picked up where he left off. This time Jenny didn't argue.

~*~*~*~

It was well past lunch time when Trevor and Jenny finally did make an appearance down stairs.

"I'm starving," Jenny said with a giggle as they waited for their lunch to arrive. "I think you were trying to starve me to death."

"I thought we were living on love Sweetheart," Trevor said as he grinned unrepentantly, "or giving it our best shot anyway."

"You're incorrigible," Jenny laughed.

"That's not the first time you accused me of that," Trevor told her still grinning.

"And I can see that nothing has changed," Jenny retorted with a roll of her eyes and a smile.

"Would you want it to?" Trevor teased.

"Not really," Jenny laughed. "What are we going to do today?"

"You mean besides go back to our room?" Trevor asked waggling his brows at his new bride.

"Yes," Jenny giggled, "besides that!"

"Ummm, Nothing!" Trevor laughed. "That was pretty much my plan for the next few days!"

"Well, I guess a girl could do worse," Jenny said sending him a sexy smile.

"I thought you said you were hungry."

"I am," Jenny assured him.

~ 146 ~

"Then I suggest you save those looks for later," Trevor warned with a sensual smile of his own.

Jenny threw back her head and laughed, "Fair enough"

"You two are having far too much fun over here," Alice, Elizabeth's sister, teased as she brought them their lunch.

"Thank you Alice," Jenny beamed at the fifteen year old girl she'd been introduced to the day before.

"You're welcome," Alice beamed back.

"Yes," Trevor chimed in, "Thank you Alice."

"You're welcome too Mr. Rollins," Alice bubbled before she bounced away.

"She seems like a really sweet girl," Jenny said after the prayer was said.

"She is a sweet girl," Trevor agreed. "She's a hard worker too. I never see her idol and I've never heard her complain."

"Much like Elizabeth," Jenny said thoughtfully. "I don't think there is a sweeter person on earth than Elizabeth Chandler."

"How do you know Elizabeth?" Trevor asked.

"Well you know my past...profession," Jenny blushed and Trevor bristled.

"We'll have none of that Jenny Lynn Rollins," he informed her sternly, "there is no shame between us. Not now, not ever. Do you hear? I'm not ashamed of your past and I don't want you to be either," Trevor continued gently as he reached for her hand and received a shy smile. "Now tell me how you know Elizabeth."

"Millie and I worked the nights and slept during the days, but we both wanted to be able to enjoy the sunshine, so we decided to see if we could acquire some "respectable" clothes that would allow us to fit in with the ladies," Jenny explained. "Not that we ever did. We weren't sure that Elizabeth would even allow us entry; nevertheless let us buy any of her beautiful creations, but when we introduced ourselves and told her why we wanted them she didn't hesitate. We became fast friends. She was the first person in town to ever take the time to get to know us."

"She was the first person," Trevor repeated, "who else took the time to get to know you in this town Jenny?"

"Well...Eric and Blain, I mean Dr. Michaels I guess."

"You mean out of all the so called Christians in this town no one took the time to ask you to church, or tell you about Christ," Trevor asked in shock and then he shook his head sadly, "three people out of a whole town full."

"I guess I didn't see it that way," Jenny admitted softly.

"Jenny, I want to make a difference," Trevor said passionately. "Not just to Christian people either! I want to be like Christ! I want to be the preacher that isn't afraid to go into the bars and sit with the sinner just so he can hear about God's saving grace. I want to be fearless in my witness for Christ!"

Jenny had never heard someone so passionate about anything before and that it was her husband talking about wanting to serve God just made it that much more inspiring.

"Oh Trevor," Jenny said as she fought back tears, "There are so many out there like me, Millie, and even Bobby and Darby."

"Who are Bobby and Darby?" Trevor asked then had to fight his own tears as Jenny told him about the fate of Adam's parents. "Where is the boy now?"

"I assume he's still at the Honky Tonk," Jenny admitted sadly.

"Not for long," Trevor told her as his eyes took on a look of steel. "I know this is our honeymoon Sweetheart, but I can't just sit…"

"Oh Trevor," Jenny squealed with delight. "Have I ever told you how wonderful I think you are?"

"You mean you don't mind if…"

"Are you kidding?!" Jenny asked, "You couldn't have given me a better wedding gift! I can't tell you how much Bobby's been on my heart."

"Well then," Trevor said getting to his feet, "what are we waiting for? I'll take you up to the room and you can wait there while I…"

"No Trevor," Jenny interrupted, "I'm your wife and since we are one this is our ministry. I want to work for the Kingdom by your side. Where you go I go."

"See, I told you you'd make the perfect preacher's wife," Trevor chuckled as he offered his wife his arm. "Well, let's get a move on then."

~*~*~*~

It was a glorious spring afternoon as Trevor and Jenny made their way across town toward the Honky Tonk. Not much was happening outside in front of the rundown building. Of course that would be a different story when the sun went down.

"Howdy, Mr. what can I...Miss Jenny!" Bobby exclaimed as he laid the broom he'd been sweeping with aside. "What are you doing here? Is the baby okay?"

"Your son is doing wonderful," Jenny rushed to assure him. "I found him a wonderful couple."

"Oh thank the Lord," Bobby breathed. "That was Darby's biggest concern when she realized that..."

"I know," Jenny said laying a gentle hand on his arm. "I'm so sorry for your loss."

"Me too," Bobby replied around the lump in his throat. "I miss her."

"I'm sure you do," Jenny said as tears filled her eyes.

"I can't thank you enough for what you did for us," Bobby smiled at her.

"It was as honor to be entrusted with such a precious gift," Jenny told him. Then she turned around and smiled up at Trevor. "Bobby I would like to introduce you to someone. This is Trevor Rollins."

"It's a pleasure to meet you Mr. Rollins," Bobby said as he shook Trevor's hand. "Any friend of Miss Jenny's is a friend of mine."

"It's a pleasure to meet you too," Trevor replied as he returned the hand shake.

"Actually, Trevor is a little more than my friend," Jenny laughed. "As of yesterday he's my husband."

"That's wonderful!" Bobby exclaimed as he shook Trevor's hand again and gave Jenny a quick hug. "Congratulations to you both."

"His brother is Adam's adoptive father," Jenny explained.

"Who's Adam," Bobby asked in confusion.

"Adam is your son," Jenny told him and watched as tears entered Bobby's eyes.

"Adam," he sighed. "I love it."

"Adam Quincy Rollins," Trevor elaborated.

"If me and Darby had been able to pick out a name for our son it couldn't have been finer," Bobby assured them with a watery smile.

"We actually didn't come here just to tell you about Adam," Jenny admitted.

"That's right," Trevor chimed in, "we were hoping to talk you into accompanying us back to Riverview."

"But…why?" Bobby asked in confusion.

"Have you ever considered blacksmithing?" Trevor asked.

"Not really," Bobby admitted.

"Well you've got the build for it and I happen to know where a position will be coming available to be Mr. Allen's apprentice in Riverview," Trevor explained.

"You know," Bobby smiled, "I think I would like that. Darby and I prayed before she died that God would show me a way out of here."

"A way out of where?" a bald, rolling fat man demanded as he entered the saloon.

~ 151 ~

"Dad, this here is Mr. and Mrs. Rollins," Bobby introduced, "Mr. and Mrs. Rollins this is my dad, Harry."

"What do you want," Harry said in way of greeting.

"Dad!"

"I've come to offer your son a position in Riverview," Trevor told him without flinching.

"He already has a position here with me," Harry informed him. "I think you need to leave."

"I'm going with them Dad," Bobby told him.

"No, you're not!" Harry bellowed. "YOU," he yelled pointing to Trevor, "take your whore and get out!"

Trevor's fist was in the other man's face before anyone could register he'd moved.

"If you know what's good for you mister," Trevor warned to the man holding his nose on the floor, "you'll refrain from talking about my wife that way."

"You broke my nose," Harry whined.

"I'll break more than that if you ever talk about Jenny that way again," Trevor promised.

"Good bye Dad," Bobby said sadly.

"If you leave don't bother coming back," Harry spat.

"Sorry you feel that way," Bobby replied as he followed Jenny and Trevor out the door.

"Go on then!" Harry bellowed as he staggered to his feet. "I was daft for claiming you as my own!"

"What?" Bobby stopped just short of the door and whirled toward the man who'd raised him.

"That's right," Harry went on ruthlessly, "I ain't your dad and I don't even know who your mother was. I found you abandoned in one of my upstairs rooms."

"Actually," Bobby replied in awe, "I'm glad I'm not yours. You never loved me anyway, and now I know there's something wrong with you. Not me."

Harry was so angry he was shaking with furry. "Get out you little b…"

"Gladly," Bobby replied as he strolled out the door without a backwards glance.

"I'm sorry Bobby," Jenny said softly when he joined them outside.

"I'm not," Bobby assured her. "I meant what I said. I'm more relieved than anything. Now I'm free to hate him for what he did to Darby."

"I'm afraid that's not how it works," Trevor told him. "But we'll talk about that later."

~*~*~*~

Once back at the hotel Trevor paid for Bobby to have a room for the night.

"Thanks Mr. Rollins," Bobby said bashfully, "I'm a hard worker and I'll pay you back."

"There's no need," Trevor assured him, "and please call me Trevor. We aren't too far apart in age."

"Thank you Mr.…I mean Trevor, but if it's all the same I'd like to pay you back when I can," Bobby told him. "I've always been a hard worker, but Dad…I mean Harry never paid me for any of it; said it was his right for taking care of me."

"Well, you're almost a grown man," Trevor told him, "you don't need him to take care of you, and you don't have to work for free."

"That's right," Jenny agreed. "I'd always heard that Harry was a bad man, but I just never expected to find...well to find such a low life."

"He's always been like that," Bobby admitted. "He doesn't like anyone. Not even himself."

"I'm just glad that you agreed to come with us," Jenny beamed at him.

"Are you sure that this Mr. Allen fellow will hire me?" Bobby asked Trevor uncertainly.

"I'm fairly certain he will," Trevor assured him. "If not we'll find you some other work."

"Where will I live?" Bobby asked as the thought occurred to him.

"Now don't you worry about that," Trevor replied. "There's a small room in back of the smithy that I used to live in that's available. It's a little cramped, but you can look for something more permanent later."

"Sounds like you have this all thought out," Bobby said with a smile. "Thank you."

"You're welcome," Trevor smiled back. "Now why don't we retire to our rooms for a couple hours and then we'll meet you in the dining room at five for dinner. You can pay me back later." Trevor added quickly before Bobby could protest.

"I'll keep track of how much I owe you," Bobby promised.

"I have no doubt of that," Trevor chuckled as the trio made their way to the stairs.

~*~*~*~

Bobby and four other people were waiting for them when they emerged down stairs shortly after five.

"Millie, Elizabeth!" Jenny exclaimed as she raced down the remaining three steps to embrace her friends.

"We were hoping we would catch you," Millie told her as she hugged her back.

"Alice said you hadn't been down for dinner yet," Elizabeth explained.

"Not yet," Jenny admitted trying to fight the blush that stained her cheeks.

"Well, we have some things we need to talk to you about," Blain addressed Trevor.

"Oh, well we were just about to get something to eat," Trevor informed him. "Would you like to join us and you can tell us about it?"

"That's what I was hoping you would say," Blain admitted with a grin.

"Me too," Eric chimed in. "Elizabeth wouldn't let me eat a thing till you joined us."

"Really!" Elizabeth said in exasperation, "You'd think he was withering away the way he's carried on!"

"I am," Eric assured her with a laugh.

"I think we better feed him then," Jenny giggled.

"Have any of you met Bobby?" Trevor asked.

"I have," Blain spoke up as he held out his hand to Bobby. "How are you Bobby?"

"Doing better Dr. Michaels," Bobby told the doctor. "I want to thank you for what you done for Darby."

"I just wish I could have done more," Blain admitted sadly.

"Harry wouldn't let me get you," Bobby said brusquely. "In truth I was shocked when you showed up."

"My wife told me about Darby," Blain explained, "I came as soon as I found out."

"Well, whatever it was you gave Darby sure helped with her pain and I can't thank you enough," Bobby told him in a thick voice.

"You know Bobby I'm glad you're here," Blain informed him. "You need to hear what we have to say too."

"What's it about?" Bobby asked in confusion.

"Let's find our table first and then we'll explain," Eric told him.

Elizabeth led the group to a small room off of the main dining room. In the center of the room sat a solitary mahogany table that would easily seat half a dozen people. Places for the couples were already set, and Alice was placing the last steaming platter on the food laden table.

"Oh, I thought Momma said six places," Alice said as she sent a shy smile toward Bobby. "I'll just go get another setting."

"I'll go grab another chair," Eric offered on his way out the door.

"I can eat in the dining room," Bobby offered.

"Nonsense," Elizabeth snorted. "You'll eat with the rest of us."

"Best not to argue with her," Eric chuckled as he carried in the seventh chair and made room at the table. "Take it from me. It doesn't do any good anyway."

"And here I thought I'd never get you trained!" Elizabeth teased as everyone took their seats.

"Here we are," Alice exclaimed as she carried in the needed items and sat them before Bobby.

"Thank you Miss," Bobby said softly.

"You're welcome," Alice replied turning a pretty shade of pink and hastily left the room.

~*~*~*~

"Okay," Blain said getting everyone's attention after they had all eaten their share, "I hate to have to bring up an unpleasant topic, but I'm afraid it's rather important."

"He's already told us," Eric added, "but we wanted to be here in case we can be of any assistance."

"You've heard that they found Jonas Monroe?" Elizabeth asked Jenny.

"Yes," Jenny replied as her gaze sought out Millie's.

"I'm fine Jenny," Millie assured her as Blain took her hand and brought it to his lips.

"Well," Blain continued still holding onto Millie's hand, "his trial is set for Friday."

"Good," Jenny exclaimed.

"They're going to charge him with rape and," Eric sent a sympathetic look toward Bobby, "murder."

~ 157 ~

"If they'd let me in the cell with him for a few minutes there wouldn't be any need for a trial," Bobby replied as his expression turned stormy.

"I feel the same way," Blain promised as he gently squeezed Millie's hand. "We'll just have to trust that the law will take care of him."

"That's why we wanted to talk to you," Elizabeth chimed in. "Jenny, we need you to testify."

"Why would you need Jenny to testify?" Trevor asked in confusion.

"Because she's an eye witness," Eric explained.

"You were there when he attacked Millie?" Trevor asked Jenny incredulously.

"No," Blain answered for her, "but she will need to tell what happened to her before she killed Travis Monroe and more importantly what Travis said."

"Okay," Trevor stood up, "what is everyone talking about."

You could have heard a pin drop as everyone around the table grew quiet and looked from Jenny to Trevor.

"He doesn't know?" Millie asked in disbelief.

"Well I haven't exactly had a chance to tell him," Jenny said as she chanced a look at her husband's confused expression.

"What haven't you had a chance to tell me?" Trevor asked still standing.

"Please sit down Trevor," Jenny asked and took a deep breath when he complied. "While Jonas attacked Millie his cousin Travis went to my room and tried to attack me, but...well I killed him with a dagger I had hidden."

No one dared breathe as Trevor digested all that had been said.

"Did you say Travis Monroe?" Trevor asked sure he'd heard wrong.

"Do you know him?" Eric asked.

"I thought he died almost a year ago," Trevor replied and everyone listened as he told them about his sister Katie.

"I can assure you," Jenny shuddered, "he was alive."

Jenny watched as the emotions played across her husband's face; disbelief, appall, anger and finally compassion as he gathered her in his arms and kissed her gently.

"I'm sorry I didn't tell you…"

"He's lucky to already be dead," Trevor said silencing her apology. "I've wanted to get my hands on Travis for quite some time for how he treated my sister Katie, but that he messed with you…well let's just say I probably wouldn't have been as kind as you were. I'm just grateful he didn't get a chance to hurt you."

"And now we need her help to make sure his cousin can't hurt anyone else ever again," Blain told them.

"Well that's up to Jenny," Trevor replied. "I'll bring her back or we can just wait here for the trial."

"Either way," Bobby spoke up, "I think it's best if I stay here for the trial."

"All of you are welcome to stay with us," Elizabeth offered.

"What do you want to do Sweetheart?" Trevor asked his bride.

"Do you need to get back to Riverview?" Jenny asked.

"No it's only two days away. We can stay," Trevor assured her.

"Why don't you bring your things over to the house in the morning," Eric suggested.

"You sure you don't mind?" Trevor asked.

"Not at all," Eric and Elizabeth assured them.

"I can find a place to stay until then," Bobby told them.

"I know you can," Elizabeth said as she gave the youth a "don't argue with me" look. "You're staying with us."

"But…"

"Remember what I told you earlier," Eric chuckled. "I'm telling you it doesn't do a lick of good."

"Guess I'll be staying with you," Bobby laughed.

Chapter 11

Friday morning dawned bright and beautiful in spite of the butterflies flying around in Jenny's stomach.

If it hadn't been for Trevor's comforting presence she was sure she wouldn't have slept at all. As it was she at least got some rest.

Jenny gazed at the man sleeping next to her and for the millionth time sent up a prayer of thanks. She snuggled closer to him and placed a gentle kiss on his chin.

"I love you so much," she whispered.

"I love you too," Trevor replied with a sleepy grin as he wrapped his strong arms around her and tucked her head underneath his chin.

Jenny sighed as she snuggled deeper into his embrace. It felt so wonderful to be in his arms protected, cherished and loved.

"Are you nervous?" Trevor's deep gravelly voice rumbled through his chest and into her ear.

"A little," Jenny admitted.

"I'll be there Sweetie," Trevor promised. "It's going to be alright."

"I just pray that justice is served for what he did to Millie and Darby," Jenny replied.

"I don't see how it can't," Trevor assured her, "sounds like there were plenty of eye witnesses."

"Well, as much as I'd love to stay and snuggle with you all day," Jenny giggled, "I'd better get dressed."

"Do we have to?" Trevor groaned as he started nibbling on her ear.

"Yes we have to," Jenny laughed as she tried to push him away.

"I'll be glad to get you home," Trevor admitted with a dramatic sigh as he let her go.

"Me too," Jenny agreed with a giggle as she got up and started to dress.

They both descended the stairs of Elizabeth and Eric's home hand in hand. Their cook already had a spread on the table for breakfast and the delicious smells made Jenny's stomach rumble in protest.

Eric, Elizabeth and Bobby were already seated around the table, but no one had made their plates yet.

"Good morning," Elizabeth said cheerfully.

"Good morning," Jenny and Trevor returned.

"Sorry we're late," Jenny told them as she and Trevor took their seats, "I didn't sleep well last night."

"I didn't either," Bobby admitted.

"I'll just be glad when all of this is over," Eric chimed in.

~*~*~*~

Breakfast had been a quiet affair and the ride to the town hall wasn't much better.

Jenny gasped out loud as they reached the makeshift courthouse. It seemed as though the entire state of Texas had turned out for the trial.

"There she is!" one man yelled and suddenly the wagon was surrounded by people.

"Miss McGreggor, is it true you had to kill the defendant's cousin?"

"Miss McGreggor, what is your relationship to Millicent Reynolds?"

"Miss McGreggor is it true that you..."

"Whoa, that's enough," Trevor commanded as he stood up and glowered at the slew of reporters crowding in to get to his wife. "Her name is Mrs. Rollins and the only time she'll be answering questions is on the witness stand."

Nonplussed the reporters turned their barrage of questions on Bobby.

"Mr. Duggard what was your relationship to Darby McFarley?"

"Mr. Duggard, why wasn't a doctor summoned?"

"Mr. Duggard..."

The men put the women in the center and plowed their way through to the door of the building. Once inside they didn't find the situation much better. Standing room was all that appeared to be left in the tiny room.

"Jenny! Elizabeth!" a familiar voice called out and Jenny saw Millie waving at her from the front row.

"We were able to procure three seats," Blain explained as they finally made their way to the front of the room. "I thought the women could sit and we men can stand by the wall."

"Thanks Dr. Michaels," Trevor smiled gratefully.

Jenny wasn't happy to be separated from Trevor, but she was grateful for a place to sit as she sat down beside Millie and Elizabeth.

It seemed like it took forever before the judge finally made his way to the makeshift stand and banged his gavel.

"Quiet down!" he demanded and the room promptly grew still. "Please bring forth the defendant."

You could have heard a pin drop as Oak Springs' sheriff dragged the giant man forward in chains and sat him before the judge.

The first witness the prosecution called was a trembling Millie. Jenny's heart broke as her friend gave her account of the awful details and then identified Jonas as her attacker.

"It was dark when you were attacked, was it not?" Jonas' attorney asked.

"There was more than enough light," Millie said softly as she shuddered with the memory.

"I'm through with this witness," the attorney said dismissing a relieved Millicent.

Next was Jenny's turn and she prayed her legs would hold her as she made her way to the witness stand. She looked for Trevor just before she gave her own account of the night's events.

"Objection Your Honor," the defense attorney interrupted, "defense would like to point out that this woman was not a witness to the actual crime and therefore her testimony has no actual bearing on this case."

"Your Honor, prosecution is trying to prove the premeditated actions of Mr. Monroe," the prosecuting attorney argued.

"Over ruled," the judge told the defending attorney.

After Jenny took her seat Bobby was called to the stand and gave his testimony. It seemed like all the cards were stacked against Jonas as the prosecution built his case, but as the testimonies were given the defendant didn't appear worried at all.

A short recess was called once the prosecution had finished calling his witnesses. Jenny desperately wanted some fresh air, but even if she was able to make it out of the building the horde of reporters that were circling outside like vultures were just waiting for someone to pounce on.

"Would the defense please call your first witness," the judge said as everyone grew silent once again.

"Your Honor the defense would like to call Horace Henderson to the stand," the attorney announced as a murmur went through the crowd. Jenny hadn't seen him since the day he'd admitted to being her biological father, and she noted that he looked weary. "Mr. Henderson, is it true that you own and operate the local saloon, and that it is indeed called Horace's Place?"

"Yes," her father confirmed, "it is."

"And isn't it also true that at the time of the alleged crime, said victim was in your employ as a prostitute?"

"No," Horace denied.

"No, she wasn't in your employ?" the attorney asked in disbelief.

"Yes, she was in my employ," Horace confirmed. "No, she was not a prostitute."

"Then what was she?" the attorney asked.

"She was a dancehall girl," her father admitted with a sigh. Everyone knew where this was going.

"So she was a lady of ill repute?" the attorney asked smugly.

"No," Horace shocked him by saying. "My girls are not allowed to be of ill repute, as you call it. I don't tolerate it."

"How can you be so sure?" the attorney asked. "In fact how do we know you yourself don't partake in the virtue of these women?"

"Objection Your Honor," the prosecuting attorney interjected.

"Sustained," the judge glared at the defense attorney. "Mr. Henderson is not the one on trial. I'll thank you to remember that."

"My apologies Your Honor," the defense attorney said contritely. "Mr. Henderson, were you with your girls every hour of the day and night?"

"Of course not," Horace snorted.

"Then it seems to me that it is quite possible for your "girls" to do as they please," the attorney argued, "and aren't they paid to dance and flirt with the men that frequent your establishment in hopes of procuring their money?"

"Yes," Horace growled.

"No further questions Your Honor," the defense attorney said dismissing the saloon owner. "The defense would next like to call Harry Duggard to the stand."

Jenny heard Bobby gasp as Harry took the stand.

"Mr. Duggard, is it true that you own the Honky Tonk at the edge of town?"

"Yes it is," Harry said puffing out his chest in a show of pride.

"In your expertise Mr. Duggard would you say that it is possible for a woman to work a saloon and still keep her virtue?" the defense attorney crooned.

"Course not!" Harry snorted.

"Would you say it was possible for someone such as yourself to refrain from partaking in said virtue?"

"I know I never could," he chortled then added, "heck my boy over there couldn't either!"

Jenny wanted to physically hurt the man on the stand as every eye in the room was turned toward Bobby.

"Are you saying that the young Mr. Duggard had relations with one of the ladies in question?"

"Sure did," Harry laughed like it was a big joke, "begged me to marry Darby he did, but I told him weren't no need for that. He could have a piece of her anytime he wanted, and believe me he did too!"

"Mr. Duggard," the judge yelled as he banged his gavel to silence the crowed, "I'll thank you to refrain from such talk. There are ladies present."

"Sorry Your Honor," the defense said trying to sound contrite. "Defense has no further questions for this witness."

The last witness called was Millie's husband, Dr. Michaels.

"Dr. Michaels," the defense attorney began, "is true that you examined Darby McFarley before she passed away?"

"Yes it is," Blain answered.

"Is it true that upon examination you learned that Miss McFarley had given birth just a few days before her attack?"

"That is confidential," Blain growled.

"Your Honor, please instruct the witness to answer," the defense attorney demanded.

"Please answer the question Dr Michaels," the judge commanded.

"Yes," the doctor answered begrudgingly, "she had."

The entire room erupted and the judge once again had to quite them down.

The remainder of the trial didn't seem real as the defense attorney argued that in the eyes of society and the expression of the law, rape of a prostitute was deemed impossible. She had already been soiled by her own actions; she had no honor to protect and therefore could not be raped.

The despicable man also argued that with Darby having given birth only days before resuming her "duties" had injured her own person. That there was no way to prove his client's actions had caused her death.

Jenny felt like she was going to be physically sick as the judge passed the verdict of not guilty, and in doing so set the rapist and murder free.

Millie passed out cold. Jenny caught her head before it could hit the floor and in an instant all four men had the women surrounded.

"I know a way out through the back," Blain offered as he gently gathered his wife in his arms.

"I'll lead the way," Bobby growled already heading that way. "Trust me, no one wants to get in my way right now."

Blain followed after him with Millie still unconscious in his arms, while Trevor and Jenny, and Eric and Elizabeth brought up the rear.

Everyone breathed a sigh of relief as they exited the building and didn't see any photographers camped out back.

"Why don't we take the women to my place and then we'll come back and get your wagon Eric," Blain suggested.

"Sounds like a plan," Eric agreed as they helped the women into the wagon and headed away from the pandemonium.

~*~*~*~

Jonas watched as the wagon headed away from him to some unknown destination.

"Doesn't matter," he muttered to himself. "I'll find 'er, and when I do she'll pay for what she did."

The attorney had done him proud, and now he was free to avenge his cousin. Something he planned to do...soon.

Chapter 12

Riverview had never looked so good! And that was saying a lot since Jenny had, had that same thought only two weeks ago.

Trevor had wired Mr. Allen the blacksmith and asked him about Bobby. It didn't take long to receive an answer, so Bobby had headed out on the first available train to his new home and job but, she and Trevor had stayed in Oak Springs long enough to help Blain and Millie pack up. She was so excited that Millie and Blain had decided to move to Riverview. Millie had been devastated by the verdict and Blain knew she couldn't stay in Oak Springs with all the memories to haunt her. When Blain and Millie announced their intention to move Trevor had told them about Riverview's need of a doctor, and how Dr. McKinney had retired shortly after LeAnn had given birth to Aisley.

It took two days for the paperwork to go through and while they were waiting Trevor had bought a wagon for him and Jenny since they needed one anyway. Then it took another four days to get the newlyweds packed and all their belongings loaded onto the wagons. So instead of taking the train back she and Trevor had driven one wagon, while Blain and Millie drove the other. It had taken a day and a half travelling to get to Riverview from Oak Springs, but it was worth it all to have Millie with her.

Eric and Elizabeth had also decided to move to Riverview. Elizabeth wanted to raise their baby in a small town setting. Eric already had a job with the bank in Riverview, but it didn't start for another week. At that time Luke and Trevor would head back to Oak Springs to help them move.

Darkness was well on its way by the time they'd gotten all the wagons unloaded and headed for their own home. Jenny laughed out loud as she realized that she didn't even know where home was.

"What was that about?" Trevor chuckled.

"It just occurred to me that I have no idea where we live," Jenny explained as she laced an arm through his, "and I don't care as long as I live there with you."

"We're almost there," Trevor promised as he placed a soft kiss on her forehead.

True to his word they were pulling up to their "home" before she knew it.

"Trevor," Jenny giggled, "this is where the school house used to be."

"Actually," Trevor said as he leapt from the wagon and reached for her, "this is the schoolhouse. After they built the new one they were going to tear this one down, but it was all I had left of you. I couldn't bear to see our memories destroyed, so I bought it and remodeled it."

"Oh, Trevor," Jenny breathed as she took in the cute little schoolhouse turned country cottage in the fading light. He had added onto the building to make it big enough to be a home, and had built a wraparound porch that sported a front porch swing. White shutters graced the many windows that would let in the cheery sunshine. It looked nothing like the building she remembered, and yet...it did.

"Do you like it?" Trevor asked as he watched her closely.

"No," Jenny smiled at him, "I love it."

"I did everything with you in mind," Trevor admitted.

"I love you Trevor Lee Rollins," Jenny sighed as she wrapped her arms around his neck. "Have I told you that?"

"Not in the last hour," Trevor teased as he claimed her lips and then lifted her into his arms.

Jenny laughed as her husband carried her across the threshold, kicked the door shut and didn't stop until he laid her on their marriage bed.

"Aren't you tired?" Jenny giggled.

"Honey," Trevor chuckled as he looked down on his precious wife, "I'll never be that tired."

~*~*~*~

Trevor and Jenny didn't even attempt to emerge from their home for three days, and the only reason they did then was because it was Sunday.

"I imagine Mom will expect us for dinner after services today," Trevor warned as he finished buttoning his shirt.

"Sweetheart, do you think you could talk to her about us inviting Millie, Blain, and Bobby for dinner?" Jenny asked as she did her hair. "Millie's like a sister to me and they don't have any other family."

~ 172 ~

"I'll ask," Trevor chuckled, "but trust me my mom will have them adopted as her own before the week is out, so we won't have to worry about asking every time. It will just be assumed they're coming."

"You're mother really is an amazing woman," Jenny told him sincerely.

"I agree, but do you know who else I think is an amazing woman?" Trevor asked as he pulled her into his embrace.

"Hummm," Jenny teased, "let me see…"

"You silly!" Trevor laughed as he placed a kiss on her lips, then her chin, cheeks, nose and eyes. "We better head for the church, or you're going to make us late."

"Me?!" Jenny gave an unlady like, "You're the one who can't behave himself."

"How am I supposed to behave myself with all this temptation in front of me," he teased as he bent down to nibble her ear.

"Try," Jenny laughed as she escaped from him and flew out the door. Trevor was right behind her, and swatted her bottom playfully as she scrambled into the wagon to escape him.

"You'll pay for that later," Trevor promised as he climbed into the wagon and laid a big one on her.

"I'm gonna hold you to that," Jenny laughed.

"Honey, you can count on it," Trevor chuckled as he set the wagon in motion.

The church yard was full of people gathered for the service. Trevor parked their wagon and helped Jenny down as his parents approached.

"I was so thrilled when Luke told us the news," Ruby exclaimed as she embraced her new daughter in law. "Not exactly surprised mind you, but thrilled."

"I *was* surprised," Jenny laughed, "but I've never been so happy."

"Me either," Trevor agreed as he wrapped an arm around her shoulders and tucked her beside him.

"We're happy for both of you," Seth chimed in.

As the couples made their way across the church lawn Jenny spotted Millie and Blain riding up in their wagon. She didn't even have to say a word as Trevor steered her their way.

"Millie!" Jenny exclaimed as she hugged her friend. "How do you like your new home?"

"I love it," Millie bubbled. "It's perfect! How do you like yours?"

Jenny explained how Trevor had bought and remodeled the schoolhouse as they walked arm in arm toward the church house, leaving the men to follow in their wake.

"How romantic," Millie said dreamily. "I think that's one of the sweetest things I've ever heard."

"I thought so too," Jenny agreed as she sent an admiring look toward her husband.

"Jenny!" two feminine voices called out Jenny spotted Katie and LeAnn waving her over.

"Oh! Millie I want to introduce you to my new sisters," Jenny said dragging her toward the other women.

"We were so excited when Lance and Luke told us the news," Katie exclaimed as she embraced her new sister in law.

"I couldn't believe it," LeAnn admitted as she hugged Jenny as best as she could with a sleeping Adam in her arms.

"How is my sweet little nephew doing?" Jenny crooned as LeAnn handed her the dozing infant.

"He is the best baby!" LeAnn enthused as she proceeded to tell them all about her new son. "Aisley is so good with him. She lets us all know he's her baby."

"She is such a doll," Jenny laughed. "Where is she anyway?"

"Her daddy has her," LeAnn replied pointing to where Luke was standing with the other men.

"I want to introduce both of you to someone," Jenny told them. "This is Millie Michaels. She's more like a sister to me than a friend. Millie this is Katie Thomas and this is LeAnn Rollins."

"It's a pleasure to meet you both," Millie said shyly.

"You're the new doctor's wife," LeAnn exclaimed.

"Yes I am," Millie said proudly.

"Well, if you're a sister to Jenny then you're a sister to us," Katie informed her as she gave her a quick hug.

"That's right," LeAnn agreed also hugging Millie. "I always wanted a sister growing up and now I have five!"

"Me too," the other women said in unison.

"I can't wait for Elizabeth to get here!" LeAnn said enthusiastically.

"Then we'll be complete," Millie laughed.

"Well almost," Katie interjected, "we'll still be missing Alice."

"I just love Alice," Jenny admitted.

"Me too," LeAnn agreed.

"Who is Alice?" Millie asked.

"She's the waitress from the Lonestar Hotel restaurant," Jenny explained. "She's Elizabeth's sister."

"Oh! I should have known," Millie exclaimed, "she's the spitting image of Elizabeth."

"All accept her eyes," Katie agreed.

"I could be mistaken," Millie said conspiratorially, "but I think she has a crush on Bobby."

"I noticed it too," Jenny giggled. "She sure did appear flustered when she went near him."

"Who's Bobby?" LeAnn asked.

"You haven't met him?" Jenny asked in dismay.

"Would you ladies like to join the rest us for church?" a male voice asked and all four women turned to find their husbands grinning at them and the rest of the yard empty.

"Oh!" four feminine voices exclaimed in unison and then laughed with the men.

"Trevor, have you seen Bobby?" Jenny asked her husband.

"Come to think of it...no," Trevor frowned.

"Who is Bobby?" Luke asked.

"You haven't met him?" Trevor asked looking back toward town.

"No, should I have?" Luke asked.

"Well...ummm...he's been here for almost two weeks," Trevor explained as he absently rubbed the back of his neck. "I just figured you would have met him by now."

"Okay...out with it little brother," Luke told him. "What is it about this Bobby guy that has you worried?"

"I'm not exactly worried," Trevor informed him. "I was just hoping you would have met him by now. You see he's well...he's Adam's biological father."

Both of the adoptive parents gasped in unison and LeAnn reached for her son cuddling him close.

"He's not here to take Adam is he?" Luke said in shock.

"No, no nothing like that," Trevor assured them both before Jenny jumped in to explain about Bobby and Darby.

"Oh the poor boy," LeAnn said sadly. "Luke, we need to find him."

"I agree Sweetheart," Luke replied wrapping his arm around his wife's shoulders.

"We'll all go together after the service," Trevor assured them.

"Katie and I will take Dr. Michaels and his wife with us to Mom and Dad's," Lance offered. "I don't think it is wise to overwhelm the boy."

"I agree," Blain chimed in. "That boy's been through a lot already. He's probably nervous to meet the couple that's adopted Adam."

"Then we'll head on over to the smithy's after the service," Luke addressed Trevor.

"Well, if we don't get ourselves into the church soon there may not be any more of the service left for us to attend," Trevor laughed.

The last hymn was being sung by the time the four couples made their way into the church, trying to be as inconspicuous and possible.

"So glad you decided to join us," Bro. Andrews teased as he took his place behind the podium.

~*~*~*~

After the service let out Trevor, Jenny, Luke and LeAnn made their way over to the blacksmith's to find Bobby. He wasn't hard to locate since he was in the shop hammering away on a horseshoe.

"Good morning Bobby," Trevor called as he and Jenny made their way to where he was working. Luke and LeAnn had decided to stay outside so Trevor and Jenny could prepare him for the introductions.

"Good morning," Bobby called back as he laid his hammer aside and smiled at the couple in front of him.

"We missed you at church this morning," Jenny told him sincerely.

"I've never been to church," Bobby admitted shyly. "Guess I'm just a little nervous."

"I understand," Trevor assured him. "I felt the same way the first time I attended a service."

"Yah, but you weren't as old as me," Bobby replied.

"Actually, I was the very same age you are," Trevor surprised him by saying. "I was sixteen years old the first time I darkened the door of the church."

"Really?"

"Really," Trevor nodded.

"It's more than just the church though," Bobby explained as tears filled his eyes.

"We know," Jenny said softly as she laid a gentle hand on his arm, "but you can't avoid it forever Bobby, and I think it would do your heart good to meet them."

"But what if they don't want to meet me?" Bobby said softly. "What if they don't want me to be a part of his life?"

"It won't be like that," Trevor assured him. "My brother and his wife are wonderful parents and they know that it's impossible for a child to have too many people that love him in his life."

"My heart broke the day Mrs. Jenny carried him away, but I knew it was the best thing I could do for him, I know it still," Bobby told them as tears made trails down his face, "but I would love to be a small part of his life. I'm just afraid they won't let me."

"Why don't you meet them for yourself and see," Jenny suggested.

"They're waiting right outside," Trevor offered.

"You mean...they want to meet me?" Bobby asked incredulously.

"Yes, we do," Luke said as he stepped into the shop holding Aisley followed by his wife carrying their son. "I'm Luke and this is my wife LeAnn."

"I…" Bobby couldn't seem to get any words to come out as he stared at the beautiful woman holding his son.

"Would you like to hold him?" LeAnn asked as tears streamed down her face.

"Please," Bobby managed as he accepted the tiny bundle. It took a while for him to get his emotions under control. "I thought I would never see him again."

"We want you to be a part of our family," LeAnn assured him.

"My baby," a little voice spoke up and everyone looked to the little girl in Luke's arms smiling proudly as she pointed at her brother.

"That's right Sweetheart," Bobby assured her as he handed Adam back to his mother. "He's your baby."

"We would like for you to come out to the family homestead and eat with us," Luke told him.

"Oh, I don't know," Bobby said uncertainly.

"Please," LeAnn pleaded. "If you're going to be part of our family you need to be prepared to join us for church services and Sunday lunches."

"You…really don't mind?" Bobby asked in amazement.

"We would be heartbroken if you didn't," LeAnn assured him.

"My brother was right," Luke told him. "There's no such thing as too much love, especially when it comes to children."

"Then I'd be honored," Bobby smiled at them both. "I want you to know though that *you* are his parents. I would never try to take him from you."

"Thank you," Luke told him as he clapped the boy on the back. "That means a lot."

"Maybe you can't be his father," Trevor told him, "but seems to me that being an uncle is the next best thing."

"I would love that," Bobby admitted.

"In that case welcome to the family," Jenny laughed as she hugged him.

"I have a family," Bobby said in awe. "I've always wanted a family."

"Wait till mom gets a hold of you," Trevor said dramatically rolling his eyes and Luke laughed along.

"Oh yah, she's gonna love you," Luke assured him.

~*~*~*~

"Bobby I insist you move in with us," Ruby demanded. "A sixteen year old boy has no business being on his own. Tell him Seth."

"You're welcome here Son," Seth agreed.

"I can stay in the smithy's apartment," Bobby assured them. "I don't mind."

"That's no place for a boy," Ruby argued. "You can move in with us and help Allen out a few days a week. We'll give you a horse to come and go with. Won't we Seth?"

"It's no use fighting her Son," Seth chuckled.

"But I really don't want to be a burden on…"

"Nonsense," Ruby snorted. "We want you here. Don't we Seth?"

"I sure could use a hand with the harvest," Seth admitted. "I had help last year, but I lost him when he married my daughter."

"Well...if you need the help," Bobby said hesitantly, "and if I won't be in the way..."

"You won't," Ruby bubbled, happy to have another chick to look after, "right Seth?"

"Right," her husband laughed.

"Alright," Bobby agreed with a grin.

"Seth will take you to get your things after everyone leaves. Won't you Honey?" Ruby asked smiling sweetly at her husband.

"Sure will," Seth agreed winking at Bobby.

Chapter 13

Thursday morning dawned bright and beautiful and Jenny watched as Trevor disappeared from view. He was on his way to get Luke and then the brothers would set off for Oak Springs where they would help Eric and Elizabeth move.

Trevor's parents had offered to let her stay with them while he was away, but Jenny was loathed to leave her new home. It was the first real home she'd had since her parents had died. The history behind it just made it all the more special to her.

Jenny had just started her spring cleaning when a knock sounded at the door, but when she opened it no one was there. Thinking she was just hearing things Jenny just shrugged it off and went back to cleaning, but when it happened again she started getting a little perturbed. By the third time a knock sounded at the door Jenny was ready to put a stop to the foolish game.

"Who is there?!" Jenny shouted as she threw open the door.

"Whoa," Lance chuckled as he held up his hands, "it's just me."

"Oh," Jenny exclaimed, "I'm sorry Lance, but someone keeps knocking on my door, but when I open it they hide."

"Sounds like a couple of mischievous school boys to me," Lance told her.

"Probably so," Jenny agreed, "but I do wish they would go bother someone else now."

"Why don't I take a look around and see if I can find any sign of the little rascals," Lance suggested.

"I would really appreciate that," Jenny said gratefully.

"No problem," Lance assured her on his way out the door," I promised Trevor I'd keep an eye on you."

"He's so silly," Jenny replied, but in truth she found her husband's concern endearing.

Jenny had just finished washing the last of the windows when Lance came back in.

"Jenny, I'm afraid I need you to come with me," he told her and Jenny felt the hair on the back of her neck stand on end.

"Why?" she asked.

"I took a look around the house and there aren't any child sized foot prints," he explained.

"Well then maybe I'm just hearing things," Jenny offered, but knew she had heard every knock.

"I don't think so," Lance told her gravely. "I found plenty of man sized footprints around the place, and from the looks of them it's a big man."

"Couldn't they be Trevor's?" Jenny asked knowing they weren't.

"I'm sorry Jenny," Lance said softly, "but I don't think they're Trevor's and I promised him I'd watch over you."

"Oh, alright," Jenny sighed sadly.

It didn't take Jenny long to gather a few clothes and toiletries.

"All set?" Lance asked.

"I guess so, but I really hate to let someone run me out of my home," she said sourly.

"I understand," Lance assured her as he reached for her bag. "Trevor will be home in a few days, so you won't be away long."

"Thanks Lance," Jenny said sincerely. "I appreciate your help."

"What are brothers for?" Lance smiled as he held the door open for her.

Neither one saw the man standing just outside the door with a raised club. Jenny screamed as Lance's knees buckled under the blow and he hit the ground hard.

"If you don't want me to kill him I suggest you do as I say," Jonas growled.

~*~*~*~

The days were getting warmer as summer sped toward the central Texas border town. Bobby had just finished work and was on his way to check on Jenny before heading home.

"Home," Bobby said the word out loud and smiled to himself. He'd never had a home before much less a real family, but Ruby had insisted that he could call her Momma and he had found it came rather natural. He and Seth laughed over the way she babied him, but in truth nothing had ever felt so good.

No one had ever truly cared for him before Darby, and he soaked it in like a sponge.

"Oh Darby, I wish you could see the family that has our son," he whispered as he headed toward Trevor and Jenny's cottage. "You would have loved them."

Trevor was still engrossed in his thoughts when he literally stumbled across the unconscious Lance. His heart dropped to the pit of his stomach and then picked up pace as he scanned the area.

"Mrs. Jenny," he called out, but no one answered. "Oh Lord, please no."

Bobby wasn't sure if it was safe to move the unconscious man so he took off at a dead run for the doctor. He had wanted to stretch his legs a little, so he hadn't brought his new horse, but his long legs ate up the ground easily and he was bursting through Dr. Michaels' office in record time.

"Doc, come quick!" he yelled.

"Bobby!" Blain exclaimed, "What's wrong?"

"Lance has been knocked unconscious and Mrs. Jenny is missing."

"Jenny!" Millie cried as she emerged from the back room.

"We'll find her Sweetheart," Blain promised. "First I have to see to Lance. Bobby could you please head over to the sheriff's office and let him know, then I need you to send a telegram to Oak Springs. Trevor needs to know."

"Yes sir," Bobby replied already on his way out the door.

~*~*~*~

Both men had wanted to make it to Oak Springs by night fall, but a broken wheel had them running behind and with darkness descending they knew they had to stop for the night.

"I hated to have to leave Jenny," Trevor sighed and Luke laughed.

"Trust me," his brother teased, "it doesn't get any better. You'd have thought I was leaving for a year the way me and LeAnn carried on."

"I hope it doesn't," Trevor informed him. "I don't ever want to get used to being away from Jenny."

"Me either," Luke agreed, "but about LeAnn of course."

"I didn't figure you meant Jenny," Trevor laughed.

"I'm really happy for you Little Brother," Luke told him sincerely.

"Thanks Big Brother."

Trevor and Luke had just gotten settled and were about to eat when they heard a rider approaching.

"What on earth?" Luke said as both men looked in the direction the noise was coming from.

"Whoever they are, they're in a mighty big hurry," Trevor chuckled.

Both men strained in the fading light to make out the figure tearing down the trail at a reckless pace.

"Is that Eric?" Trevor asked as the rider got closer.

"What on earth is he doing out here at this time of the evening?" Luke asked.

"Something must have happened," Trevor said as a sinking feeling entered his gut.

"Trevor!" Eric shouted when he was close enough to be heard. "You gotta go back! Jenny's missing!"

"What?" Luke asked in confusion, but Trevor was already on his feet and gathering his things.

"Take my horse," Eric offered as he jumped off the animal. "Luke and I will ride the rest of the way to Oak Springs and get some mounts of our own."

Trevor didn't even bother with a thank you as he mounted Eric's horse and flew back down the road at breakneck speed.

"Father, please let her be alright," he pleaded.

~*~*~*~

Jenny had never been so scared in her life. She knew there was little hope she would come out of this alive.

Jonas hadn't said a word to her since he'd abducted her, and that had been hours ago. He finally stopped beside a river and shoved her off of his horse. Jenny hit the ground hard and she cried out as pain exploded down her right side.

"That ain't nothing," Jonas chuckled, "wait until you see what I have planned for you tomorrow."

"Why tomorrow?" Jenny ground out hotly as she picked herself up off the ground.

"Because we're gettin' close to Indian Territory missy and while I'm more than ready to let them have your hide, I'd like to keep mine," he sneered as he set about making a camp fire.

~ 188 ~

"Indians," Jenny squeaked as she looked around nervously. She'd heard horror stories of what the Indians could do to a white woman.

"Now see, that's the precise reaction I was hoping for," Jonas chuckled. "I've been trying to think up an appropriate punishment for you. Naturally if you were any other woman I'd just do the deed myself, but since I feel absolutely no desire for you, what with you murdering my cousin and all, I'll have to find a more willing substitute."

"Why not just kill me?" Jenny threw at him.

"I'm not going to let you off that easy," Jonas snorted.

"Jonas, what was I supposed to do?" Jenny asked. "Let him attack me?"

"It was his right," Jonas informed her. "You're nothing, but a whore, and he had every right."

"You're lucky her husband's not here to hear you call her that," a masculine voice said startling both of them.

"Bobby!" Jenny cried as she ran to his side.

"You're never gonna hurt another woman again," Bobby informed the other man as he pulled the hammer back on his .45.

"Bobby, you can't just shoot him," Jenny said gently.

"She's right Boy," Jonas laughed. "I would hate to see you go to jail for murder. I'm not a whore, so it would be a little harder to get by with it than it was for me."

"You're nothing but a low down coward," Bobby growled. "You'd rather beat up on women than to actually face a real man."

"You think you're man enough to take me Boy," Jonas taunted.

"No," Bobby answered, "I know I'm man enough."

"Then what are we waitin' for?" Jonas jeered.

"No Bobby!" Jenny pleaded. "It's a trick."

"I'm ready when you are old man," Bobby said as he handed Jenny his gun. "If he tries anything shoot him."

"Please don't do this Bobby," Jenny begged.

"I have to," Bobby said softly. "I have to do this for Darby."

Jenny watched as the two men circled one another; each sizing the other man up. Jonas was the first to throw a punch, but it hit nothing but air as Bobby easily sidestepped the slow, giant brute, and then delivered a punch of his own that connected with the other man's ribs.

Jonas grunted as pain shot through his ribs, but Bobby showed the other man no mercy as he delivered two more blows; one to his gut and then his face.

Jenny watched as Jonas fell to his knees.

"What a joke," Bobby sneered as he spat beside Jonas. "You're nothing but a big wimp."

"You've just signed your death warrant Boy," Jonas chuckled as he pulled a derringer out of his boot.

"Bobby!" Jenny screamed.

What happened next was a blur as Bobby pulled out a derringer of his own and three shots went off almost simultaneously.

Jenny looked around for where the third shot came from and gasped when a familiar figure emerged from the shadows.

"Horace!"

"Are you hurt Jenny?" Horace asked running to her side and pulling her into his embrace still aiming his rifle at the now dead man.

"No, but," Jenny turned toward Bobby and saw him lying on the ground next to Jonas. "Bobby!"

~*~*~*~

Trevor heard the shots and dug his heals into Duke's flanks. Horse and rider flew in the direction of the sound and camp fire light.

Trevor dismounted and pulled out his .45 as he crept up on the makeshift camp sight.

"Jenny!" Trevor exclaimed as he stepped out of the shadows.

"Trevor!" Jenny cried as she flew into his arms.

"Oh Sweetheart, I've never been so scared in my life," Trevor told her as he held her.

"Trevor, Bobby's been shot," Jenny said pulling away and racing back to the boy's side.

"Bobby," Trevor called gently as he examined his wound.

"I'm alright," Bobby grimaced as Trevor poked at his shoulder. "His aim was as bad as his fighting."

"You fought him?" Trevor asked in astonishment as he looked to where Jonas' lifeless body was sprawled out.

"I knew I couldn't just shoot him in cold blood," Bobby explained as he struggled to sit up, "so I challenged him and when he realized he couldn't beat me he pulled out a derringer."

"The coward couldn't just fight like a man," Jenny snorted disdainfully.

"I've never been so scared in my life," Horace spoke up grabbing everyone's attention.

"How did you know?" Jenny asked in confusion.

"Well...I sold the saloon and wanted to try one more time to make amends with you," Horace admitted, "but when I got to Riverview everyone was in a panic. Dr. Michaels said you were missing and so I tracked you here."

"I...I don't know what to say," Jenny admitted trying to digest it all.

"Well, I think we're going to have to save all that for later, but for right now we need to get Bobby to Dr. Michaels ," Trevor informed them. "I'll let the sheriff know where he can find Jonas."

"First we need to pack and wrap the wound to try to stem the flow of blood," Jenny surprised them all by saying as she started ripping strips of cloth from one of her petticoats.

With Trevor's help she bandaged Bobby and made him a makeshift sling from one of her strips.

After Trevor and Horace helped Bobby onto his horse Trevor tied the reigns of Jonas' horse to his saddle horn.

"I can ride Jonas' horse," Jenny offered.

"You are riding with me," Trevor informed her, his tone brokering no argument.

"A girl could do worse," Jenny teased as Trevor swung up into his saddle and then lifted her onto his lap.

"A man could too," Trevor teased back as he bent down and tenderly kissed her lips.

It was beginning to break day light by the time the four of them started toward Riverview without a backwards glance at the man still lying in the dirt.

~*~*~*~

Lance was just leaving Blain's office when they road up to the building.

"Lance!" Jenny cried scrambling off of Trevor's lap and horse to hug her brother in law. "I've been so worried about you. Are you okay?"

"Yah, he just hit my head," Lance laughed. "Might have been much worse if he'd hit me somewhere else."

"Your head is the thickest part of your body," Trevor teased.

"Nonsense," Jenny scolded, but she couldn't hold back a giggle.

"Lance, would you mind helping me get Bobby into the doctor's office," Trevor asked, "and then I was hoping you wouldn't mind taking Jenny to the homestead."

"Trevor, I want to go home," Jenny protested.

"No Jenny, you'll be safer with my parents," Trevor informed her in his no arguing with me tone.

"No Trevor, there is no reason for that," Jenny sassed. "I'm in no immediate danger. Jonas is dead and I want to go home."

"I could stay with her until you get there," Horace spoke up for the first time since he'd found Jenny.

"See," Jenny pounced on Horace's offer, "I'll be perfectly safe."

"I don't know Jenny," Trevor said eyeing them both doubtfully. He knew Horace was her father, but as far as he was concerned he was a lousy one.

"Trevor, Horace has been protecting me for the last six years..."

"Is that what you call it?" Trevor interrupted.

"Trevor!" Jenny said in surprise.

"No Jenny, he's right," Horace said sadly. "I haven't been a good father. Actually I've been a horrible father. I've had to protect you because I kept putting you in situations where you needed protecting. I should have sold the saloon the night I saw you on the street. I knew you were mine. There was no mistaking the daughter of Matilda." Tears filled the man's eyes as he looked at his daughter, "I don't deserve you, and I definitely don't deserve your forgiveness..."

"I didn't deserve forgiveness either Horace, but God gave it to me," Jenny said softly as she laid a gentle hand on her father's arm. "I want you to know that I forgive you. I don't know when I'll be ready to call you dad...if ever, but I forgive you and I want you to be a part of my life."

"Sweetheart, that is more than I could have ever hoped for," Horace told her as he pulled her in to his arms for a fierce hug. "I want you to know that I love you Jenny. You are a wonderful woman and you deserve a much better life than what I've offered you."

"Thanks Horace," Jenny replied as she stepped back and smiled at him.

"I'm sorry for what I said," Trevor spoke up as he extended his hand toward Jenny's father.

"No need to be sorry," Horace assured him as he pumped his son in law's hand. "You were right. I'm so glad she has you. Take good care of her. She's one in a million."

"I will," Trevor replied as he tucked Jenny beside him and kissed the top of her head. "Sweetheart, are you sure you don't want to go wait for me at my parents'?"

"Trevor, I haven't had a real home since my parents died," she shot Horace an apologetic look.

"No need for that Jenny," he assured her. "They were your parents. I'm not asking to take Mr. McGreggor's place. I'm thankful that he was a good father to you."

"He was," Jenny agreed, "but I think I have enough love in my heart for you both."

"Thank you," Horace said sincerely.

"I want to go home," Jenny told her husband. "Horace can take me."

"Okay Sweetheart," Trevor agreed.

~*~*~*~

Trevor was exhausted by the time he finished up at the sheriff's office and headed toward the doctor's office to check on Bobby one more time.

"How are you feeling?" he asked the boy as he sat down in a chair next to his bed.

"I'm feeling great," Bobby answered truthfully. "Dr. Michael's gave me something for the pain, Mrs. Jenny is safe and Jonas is dead. I'm better than great."

"I wanted to thank you for what you did for Jenny," Trevor said around the lump in his throat.

"I was too late to help when they attacked Darby," Bobby said softly, "but there was no way I was going to be late again. As soon as I sent the telegraph to you I headed out. I'm just sorry I wasn't able to stop him before he took her."

"Well, I can never repay you for what you did, but if you ever need anything I'm your man," Trevor assured him.

"You and Mrs. Jenny believed in me when no one else did," Bobby informed him. "If anybody owes anybody it is I that owes you. I can't tell you how much it means to have a fresh start, but to have a family and a home…well…those things are beyond priceless. Thank you Trevor."

"You're welcome Little Brother," Trevor smiled at him and Bobby beamed back.

~*~*~*~

Jenny was glad to finally be alone with Trevor. It had been a crazy day and she was ready for some cuddling.

She still couldn't believe that she was lying in *her* bed, in *her* home with *her* husband. She had dreamed of it for so long she wondered if it would ever truly sink in.

"Did you and your father get things worked out," Trevor asked as he held her.

"Yes," she answered. "It will take some time to build a father, daughter relationship, but I think we have at least taken a few baby steps."

"I'm glad," Trevor told her sincerely.

"It seems so surreal to me that only a few weeks ago I was working in a saloon at this time of the evening," Jenny admitted. "I always hated everything about what I did."

"I'm so sorry you had to go through that Sweetheart," Trevor said as he gave her a light squeeze.

"I'm not," Jenny surprised him by saying as she propped herself up on her elbow to peer down into her husband's face. "I would never have met Millie, Bobby and Little Adam. The only regret I have is that it took me so long to make my way back to you."

"There was not a day that went by that I did not think of you," Trevor whispered as he tenderly tucked a stray strand of hair behind her ear.

"Oh Trevor," Jenny breathed as she caught his hand and placed a gentle kiss in his palm, "I missed you so much I ached."

"Well Sweetheart, the missing is over," Trevor said as he pulled her toward him, "and I'm never gonna let you go again."

"Won't be a need," Jenny giggled as Trevor started to nibble her neck. "You couldn't get rid of me now if you wanted too."

"Then it's a good thing I don't want to," Trevor teased as he claimed his wife's lips.

Epilogue

December 1896

"Mom, we're gonna be late."

"I'm almost done Matilda," Jenny informed her impatient eight year old as she put a festive, green ribbon on the end of the copper braid she just plaited down her daughter's back. "There."

"Thanks Momma," Matilda said giving her mother a quick peck on the cheek before racing from the room; practically running over her father in the process.

"Well, someone sure is in a big hurry," Trevor chuckled as he entered their bedroom.

"She can't wait to see Aisley and Brooke," Jenny laughed. "She wants to show them the new doll she got for Christmas this morning. Were you able to get clothes on James?"

"Barely," Trevor sighed dramatically. "That boy has way more energy than I've got."

"I think he has more energy than the two of us put together," Jenny laughed thinking about her rambunctious two year old. "Where are Darby and Cora?"

"They are trying to corral James," Trevor chuckled. Their five year old twin girls had a lot of energy, but even they had a hard time keeping up with their baby brother.

"I think we're all set," Jenny said turning back to the mirror one last time to check her reflection.

"It's no use," Trevor said as he wrapped his arms around his wife's waist from behind and pulled her against him. "You're beautiful no matter what you do."

"I'm glad you think so," Jenny giggled as she turned around in his arms to face him.

"It's a fact Sweetheart," Trevor assured her just before his lips claimed hers. Time stood still and everything faded away as their lips did a timeless dance.

"Ewwwwe," a tiny voice cried out and they broke the kiss to gaze down at their tiny son's scrunched up face.

"Mom, Dad we're late," Matilda whined.

"To be continued," Trevor promised as he grabbed his wife's hand and led her from the room.

~*~*~*~

The ride to the homestead didn't take long and all of their children pilled out of the wagon before Trevor had a chance to set the break.

"Well, it's about time," Luke teased as he approached the wagon.

"Yah," Lance chimed in, "We were about ready to send a hunting party out after you."

"I told y'all they would be here," Bobby defended his favorite brother as he helped Jenny from the wagon. "I am glad you made it though," he whispered to Jenny. "Alice is having a terrible time keeping little Trevor busy until James could get here."

Once Elizabeth and Eric had moved to Riverview Elizabeth's parents and sister, Alice, hadn't been too far behind. With Alice it was love at first sight, but it took Bobby a little longer to get over Darby. Once he did come around though he didn't waste any time declaring his intentions to court Alice and they had just celebrated their fifth wedding anniversary.

"Poor Alice," Jenny laughed, "I don't know what I'd do without my girl's help with James. I'll have to ask her if she wants to borrow one."

"She might just take you up on that offer," Bobby laughed, "especially now."

"Especially now," Jenny echoed trying to make sense of the odd statement, and then it dawned on her. "Bobby is Alice…"

"Shhh," Bobby chuckled. "We're going to announce it later."

"Oh Bobby I'm so excited for y'all," Jenny whispered excitedly.

"What are you two conspiring about over here?" Trevor asked.

"We are not conspiring," Jenny defended. "Will you gentlemen be so kind as to help me carry this food into the house?"

"Sure," her brothers all said in unison, but her husband sent her his "I'm on to you" look.

The house was full of loved ones as Jenny and Trevor entered the front door. Everyone was there.

"Merry Christmas Baby," Horace said as he kissed his daughter's cheek.

"Merry Christmas Dad," Jenny returned. She was so thankful that she'd chosen to have a relationship with her father. He had been true to his word about turning over a new leaf. It only took one service for him to give his life to Christ. He'd married a widow with no children of her own and together the two of them spoiled her children unmercifully.

"Ganpa!" a tiny voice demanded and both mother and grandfather looked down to find James pulling on his pants leg.

"Well hello there Jamesy Boy!" Horace cried as he swung his grandson high into the air.

"Wee," James squealed.

"Jenny!" Millie cried as she waddled through the crowed.

"Merry Christmas Millie!" Jenny replied as she met her adorably pregnant friend half way. She was due in January, but Jenny had her doubts.

"Merry Christmas," Millie laughed as she hugged her. "Come," Millie said grabbing Jenny's hand and pulling her toward the kitchen, "All of us women are in here."

"Merry Christmas Jenny," they all cried as she entered the kitchen.

Jenny hugged LeAnn, Katie, Elizabeth, Alice, Mary and Ruby as children weaved in and out of the room.

"Where is your mother?" Jenny asked LeAnn.

"Oh they'll be here," LeAnn assured her. "My mom likes to make an entrance."

Almost on cue Emily Chandler made her appearance in the kitchen and LeAnn sent Jenny an "I told you so look."

"Merry Christmas everyone," she said cheerfully.

~*~*~*~

Ruby couldn't believe how blessed she was as she looked around at her full house. Friends and family were packed in like sardines, but no one seemed to care as they laughed and cut up.

She sighed and leaned back into her husband's embrace as he wrapped his arms around her from behind.

"We sure are blessed," Seth whispered in her ear making her skin tingle all the way to her toes.

"I was just thinking the same thing," Ruby admitted.

"Papa, would you please take us fishing?"

Both grandparents turned to find a serious Blake and Adam staring up at Seth expectantly.

"Well boys," Seth chuckled, "I'd love to take you fishing, but I think it's going to snow later."

"We don't mind fishing in the snow," Blake answered obviously committed to their endeavor.

"I don't doubt that you boys are tough enough for fishing in the snow," Seth assured them, "but I'm afraid the fish won't be biting right now."

"Are they afraid of snow?" Adam asked incredulously; a comical expression on his face.

"Well, no," Seth and Ruby chuckled, "but it's too cold for them to want to move around much."

"Awe nuts," Blake said in disgust. "Now what are we gonna do for fun Adam?"

"I just don't know Blake," Adam admitted as he hung his little head. "I just don't know."

"Tell you what boys," Seth grabbed their attention by saying, "what if we went out into the barn and piled a bunch of hay under the loft for you to land on?"

"Oh yah!" they both cried in unison each taking one of their grandfather's hands. "You're the best, Papa!"

Ruby chuckled as she watched two of her grandsons drag her husband off.

~*~*~*~

"There you are," Jenny said in surprise when she found her husband alone on the porch.

"Shhh," he chuckled and tucked her beside him. "Listen."

It only took a moment before the sound of children's laughter reached her ears.

"What on earth?" Jenny giggled. "I wondered where all the children went off to."

"The children and the grandfathers," Trevor amended.

"What?" Jenny looked at him, but he just shook his head and led her to the barn's entrance. Jenny couldn't help but laugh when she peeked in the door and saw all the grandchildren romping in the hay with her dad, Trevor's dad and LeAnn's dad. The grandfather's were laughing just as hard as the children and all of them had hay everywhere. "Oh your poor dad," Jenny giggled looking at the mess that her father in law would most certainly have to clean up.

"Oh, don't feel sorry for him. He's the one who instigated the whole thing," Trevor chuckled as he led her toward the river and their favorite place on the whole ranch. Once they had reached the fallen log bench, that Trevor had proposed to her on so long ago, they both sat down in companionable silence and watched the red river meander by.

"I love you Trevor Lee Rollins," she sighed as she tilted her head up for a kiss, but she let out a little shriek as her husband pulled her onto his lap.

"And I love you Jenny Lynn Rollins," Trevor replied as he slowly closed the distance and then added just before his lips claimed hers, "unconditionally."

A note from the author

Thank you for reading Unconditional Suitor. This book was by far the most challenging for me in the Rollins of Riverview Series.

Saloons and dancehall girls weren't something I knew a whole lot about, and I was fascinated by all I learned.

Most of the shady women of the west didn't have a choice in their circumstances. A rape victim was often considered lost and deemed by the community to be of less virtue than the still "pure" women, and were therefore only fit for certain "jobs."

Jobs were scarce and even harder for a woman to find. Most made their living by prostitution, some were dancehall girls that doubled as a prostitute and some only worked the dancehalls. The dancehall girl made far more in most situations, but there were a few prostitutes that...well...made quite a bit for their...um...services.

Although their reputation was tarnished they demanded and received a lot of respect in the saloons and any man that insulted one of the girls usually had to take on the whole saloon.

Most of the women had hearts of gold and would help anyone that needed helping. During times of outbreaks they were frontline nurses.

A less than wonderful aspect I found was that by law a prostitute could not be raped according to the law. The words I used in the book at the end of the crazy trial, "in the eyes of society and the expression of the law, rape of a prostitute was deemed impossible. She had already been soiled by her own actions; she had no honor to protect and therefore could not be raped," were actually an almost word for word quote.

It makes me sad to think of all the women that found themselves in such horrible situations. I wish I could go back in time and share Christ with them, but I guess not much has changed really. There are still a lot of women out there in situations that they didn't wish for. I pray I can make a difference in their lives.

Thanks again and God bless!

www.daachristianromance.com
daachristianromance@yahoo.com

Made in the USA
San Bernardino, CA
21 March 2015